The GREATEST CHOICE

Chris Sorensen

To Elaine,

All the best!

POND
PUBLISHING

ISBN 978-0-9719423-2-5

To contact the author with questions or comments,
or if you would like to schedule him for an author signing
or speaking engagement, please contact him at:

chris@pondpublishing.com

Please also find me on the following sites:

Twitter: @csorensenwrite
GoodReads: @csorensen
Facebook: www.facebook.com/csorensenwrite

To my parents . . .

. . . for making the hard choices

The GREATEST CHOICE

When you have to make a choice and don't,

that is in itself a choice.

- William James

1

Culmination

Judge Sander's chamber door sounded like it was made of steel instead of pine as it slammed behind him. He made his way into the courtroom and took a seat at the large bench in front.

It was unusually humid. My shirt felt like it had shrunk, hugging my shoulders with a warm uneasiness. The ceiling fan that leisurely spun above was gracious enough to spread the temperate wealth. My stomach was growling, my eyes were heavy, and I was sweating more than anyone else in the room. Unfortunately, I didn't have the luxury of complaining.

The bailiff stood. "Proceedings for Lewis James Anderson held on the fifth day of July, 1954, at the Wayne County courthouse in the Commonwealth of Pennsylvania. The Honorable Judge . . ."

"Mr. Anderson," Judge Sanders squawked, interrupting the bailiff who sat down silently, seeming unfazed and used to the routine.

"Yes, your honor," I mumbled softly.

His voice was impatient. "Mr. Anderson, you had better raise your head and look at me when you answer in this courtroom."

His features came into gaze—his graying hair, broad shoulders beginning to slump a little with age, chiseled jaw and large rounded eyes. Even when he squinted his pupils were still discernable.

There was no emotion left in me as I raised my head. "Yes, your honor."

Stinging and unsympathetic the judge repositioned his bifocals and continued in his deep voice. "What did you expect to happen, Mr. Anderson? You have stood before me three times in the last five months. First you received a warning, and considering the damage to Mr. MacKay's mailbox and lawn you got off lucky. Then you were caught driving, let me see . . . oh, here it is, 'driving like a crazed maniac' in broad daylight down past the school. But what did a three-month suspension of your license do? Absolutely . . ."

I blanked out. None of the facts were new. In the past there may have been some guilt, but my feelings were numb. The beads of sweat were making their way down the small of my back. My eyes continued to gaze through Judge Sanders as I waited for the inevitable.

His eyebrows kept creeping up his forehead and his voice got louder . . . "and I should think it would stand to reason that wrapping your car around a hundred-year-old oak while driving without a license would have knocked some sense into you. Along with a fifty dollar fine, three days behind bars, and revoking your license indefinitely. I was hoping that if you missed work for a while you would realize the seriousness of your choices, but then I found out that you had no job! And now, finally, here we stand, together again," he said, finishing his dissertation with a small chuckle of disbelief.

A drop of perspiration had settled on the tip of my nose and I reached up to scratch it. I winced as I brushed my eye.

"Before we go any further Mr. Anderson, one thing that may be of interest to you, in case you can't remember. When you were pulled from the car that was in Mr. Krueger's hardware store window two days ago you were so drunk you could not even stand up long enough to have the handcuffs

2

placed on you. And that nice gash underneath your eye . . . you did that on the door getting into the patrol car."

The wreck was an event that, no matter how long I had tried over the last 48 hours, I could not remember; even though the cut above my left cheek was still throbbing. Everything was still a blur. It was the first time that I couldn't . . .

My train of thought shifted as a noticeable change came over the judge. An air of sympathy promptly transformed his stern face. The main door to the courtroom behind me squeaked close.

"Good morning, Sadie," he said slowly, almost reverently.

My head dropped. Completely sober and with a sudden rush of shame, my emotions turned on. The numbness was gone and it felt like my heart was coming up my throat.

"Morning Judge Sanders," she said quietly, politely, and then made her way down the aisle, sitting a few rows behind me. I didn't turn around to look.

Judge Sanders took in a deep breath and gently shook his head as he shuffled some papers. His hands finally stopped moving and came to rest on top of his desk. "Sadie, I sure am sorry to see you down here again. Do you know why Lewis is here today?"

The bench creaked as she stood. "Yes your honor," she stated, her voice nervous and unsure. Sadie was never one to speak in front of an audience. "I was going to Swisher's Market for Ms. Green the other day and saw the accident at the hardware store. When I saw Lewis drive by in the police car, it didn't take much to put it together." Judge Sanders nodded respectfully and Sadie sat back down. His mouth opened to speak and then he stopped to remove his glasses and massage his eyes. Sighing, he replaced his glasses and continued. "Thirty days in jail Lewis. That's all I'm going to give you for now. I'll have more for you when you're done sobering up in the county facilities."

Whatever he wanted to do was fine with me. I just wanted to get away, out of the courtroom, out of Sadie's view.

"I'll see you as soon as you get out and let you know what's next." He reached for his gavel. "Unlike some of the other men who stand before me who have been drinking all their lives, you are still fairly young. Let's see . . . twenty-seven. Is that correct Mr. Anderson?"

"Yes sir," I finally answered.

"And from everything I've gathered this apparently is a recent problem for you. You've got a chance to clean yourself up Mr. Anderson, and I suggest you take it," he finished with a drop of the gavel.

I wanted to look, but I didn't. I couldn't. The officer led me right past her and I kept my head low, wondering if I would ever see her again.

2

———

Uncertain

"Open number three," the officer shouted, his hands tightening around my bicep. The door clamored shut and the musky smell of damp, humid walls made me gag. There was going to be nothing routine about this particular visit. The thirty days that awaited me were going to be completely different than any I had ever known, or at least any that I could remember. I walked into my cell, the door slammed behind me, and for the first time it was my body—not my mind—telling me I needed a drink.

But that feeling did not last long. The guys on the inside who were long term had a system of getting anything they needed. If you wanted something bad enough you could get it. So on my fourth day of lock up, when I couldn't take it any more, Moses Johnson scored some scotch from one of the officers and gave me a couple of shots. I could feel the difference those two small drinks made. It didn't help my head as much as I would have hoped, but for a brief moment my body could manage.

With a little help from Moses every couple of days, my sentence became almost tolerable. I could handle meal times and work detail. The hardest part was after dinner, when there was nothing to do except think. No matter how bad I wanted to, there wasn't any way to escape my thoughts.

"Lewis," came the voice on the bottom bunk.

"Yeah, Henry."

"You thinking?"

"Not really Henry. Just laying here."

There was silence as Henry thought of a response. Henry was extremely slow on the uptake and had the maturity level of a young child. Everyone said he was just born that way. If asked, Henry would reply honestly that he didn't know how old he was, but it seemed he was in his mid-forties. Unlike most people who usually became annoyed with his incessant questioning and fidgeting, I could tolerate him. Mostly, I just felt sorry for him.

"I was just thinking and wanted to ask you a question." I paused to let him continue, but he was insistent on a response.

"Go ahead Henry, you can ask me," I encouraged, somewhat impatiently.

"Do you suppose you would be willing to stay in this cell with me? It's been kind of nice having somebody to talk to who don't always get mad at you. You've been pretty nice that way and I was wondering . . . I was wondering if there was any way I could talk you into staying?"

I continued to stare at the ceiling as I responded, starting slowly. "Well Henry, I wouldn't mind bunking with you, but I will be out of here in a few weeks. So I won't be staying that long."

He gave my response time to sink in and then continued, "Well, you'll probably be back later, won't you?"

His statement took me by surprise. I leaned over the bunk to look at him. "What do you mean?"

"Well the way I see it," he started, as if stating fact, "it's all downhill from here. It's not like you're really going to stop drinking, right? So whatever happens next will get you in here longer, and then the next thing longer, all the way down until you'll be able to spend all your time in here like me. I just figured I'd ask you about being cell mates now, before somebody else asked you later."

I lay back again on the cot and didn't respond. I didn't know how to respond. With all the wrangling in my mind I hadn't taken the time to think about the future, I had only been beating myself up over the past. But when Henry's question sank in and I dared to think about what would happen after I got out of jail, I couldn't help but come up with the same reasoning.

"I don't want to talk anymore Henry. Just go to sleep." He didn't say anything else.

I tried to go to sleep, but my conscience wouldn't let me. Something inside me kept gnawing at me telling me that Henry was right.

It kept me up, harping, focusing, repeating the main gist of what Henry had said, *'It's not like you're really going to stop drinking, right?'*

❖   ❖   ❖

She sat across the glass, holding her purse secure in her lap. With every few steps I took she would look at me; not in the eye, but at me and then look back down. It had been a little over three weeks since the courthouse and I had no idea what to say or what to expect. After everything I had put her through I didn't expect to see her.

As I sat in the wooden chair she finally looked me in the eyes, but her expression didn't change. Hesitantly, I picked up the phone and she followed suit. We sat in silence for a few seconds. "Hi," I began simply. She stared at me, lips firm and eyes determined. A few more seconds of silence ensued. I tried to continue.

7

"I . . . I just . . ." She held her hand up for me to stop, eyes trembling and moist. She brushed her cheek with her fingers, exhaled and took control of the conversation.

"I've had time to think Lewis, probably more than was good for me, but enough to get the job done." My mouth opened to speak, but as she slowly shook her head her eyes told me to say nothing; to sit still and listen.

"Danielle is well and she knows what's going on. I didn't see any need to stay in the house by ourselves so we are staying at your mom's.. We're going to stay there when you get out next week. You'll have the house to yourself. I've been . . ." she paused, her eyes wandering for the words. There was a swelling in my chest and I could feel a moist heat building behind my eyes.

"I've been faithful Lewis. I've been patient, kind, caring, loving, enduring—you name it. All because I believe in you. And even though I know our relationship isn't as bad as some, I think I finally figured out it is worse than most."

Her eyes became fixed and she seemed to calm to a steadier, more confident tone. "I just wanted to come to let you know that I made a promise to stop blaming myself."

As she spoke, it was as if her shoulders floated, like a weight had been lifted and dropped, dead, square at my feet. Real or not, I could feel her pain hit the floor in front of me.

My feet shuffled under the chair and I tried to make sense out of the sudden emotion, the sudden sickness I felt. "What does that mean 'you promised yourself?" I asked. For a moment I forgot I was in prison and actually, for a moment, sober, I felt like a husband again. It was a pleasant, painful sensation.

She turned away as she wiped her cheek again. There was no answer. The silence got to me.

"What do you want me to do?"

"I want you to change," she said suddenly, quickly, her voice pleading with an undertone of anger and betrayal that made me turn away. Whatever composure she came with was gone. Her voice slowly rose in tone and sharpness as she continued.

"I want you to want to change because you know you need to; not because I want you to, or your mother wants you to, or because Danielle wants you to." She slowed her tone, "not because your father would want you to." The words chosen were not meant to be spiteful, but to merely drive home her point. It worked and I became angry.

"This has nothing to do with dad," I replied loudly, deeply. The eyes around us paused to stare. The guard perked up and started toward us, but Sadie gently waved him away. Speaking into the phone again I was still angry, but hushed.

"It's not my fault that . . ."

She interrupted, boiling over, teeth clinched. "That is the point Lewis; none of this has been your fault. Quit trying to place blame and just realize everything doesn't work out all the time. I'm sorry you had to stop going to college, I'm sorry that your dad died, and I'm sorry you didn't get the job you were promised. We just have to deal with the things life throws at us. That's why I wanted to be there, so we could do it together. I told you I would always be there, but there was nothing I could do when you didn't let me in. We needed to stay together; you needed to believe in me, not run away."

"It's not that simple Sadie," I pleaded.

"It doesn't matter how it is Lewis. I have always been willing to work together, to get through it together. But you haven't let me in. I saw you struggle and didn't know what to do. You wouldn't let me do anything." She stopped and tried to gather her emotions.

Sitting there, hopeless, shoulders sagging, I knew there wasn't anything I could do.

"Judge Sanders said you get out next week. You do whatever you want Lewis. Your clothes and some food will be at the house; enough to give you something to get through the first couple of days. Danielle and I will not be there."

"Will I get to see you?"

"No, I don't want to see you, not right now. Not for a while. But, of course Danielle does. And it wouldn't be right for me to make it so you couldn't see her. But the only way you will be able to see her is if you go by mom's house while I'm at work," there was a pause, "and only if you're sober."

There was no expression on my face. Dazed, I just wanted the conversation to be over. "So this is goodbye," I said as I stood up, pitiful, still looking at the floor. I motioned to the officer to let him know I was finished.

"Wait Lewis," she said. The anger had seemed to subside a little and she was speaking from the part of her that still cared. The part of her that hoped there was still a chance. The guard noticed and halted his step. I slowly put the phone back to my ear.

"I want you to be honest with me—have you had anything to drink since you've been in here?"

I wanted to lie. Standing there, mouth half opened, she knew the answer. She looked away and I could feel her shame. I hung up the phone and the guard opened the door and proceeded to escort me back to my cell. It was the lowest point of my life.

3

Unmasking

"So," Judge Sanders began, sitting down in his swivel chair and putting on his glasses, "what is going to happen next?" He studied me and waited for an answer.

Since the talk with Sadie, I spent the remainder of my time in jail trying to pretend like I didn't care about anything. It was easy to pretend I didn't care about Sadie. She was the one that decided to leave me, right? She was the one not willing to work it out. If she wanted to give up on me then there was nothing I could do about it, right?

As much as I tried to play it off though, deep inside I still wanted to hold on to the hope that she'd be back. It was the same feeling that kept reminding me that it was actually _all_ my fault. It was because of the choices _I_ had made, not her.

So as I stood before Judge Sanders, the only course of action I had decided on was to go get drunk, do something stupid, and then head back to jail. After much contemplating, Henry's idea didn't seem all that bad.

Because I had made up my mind to give up, I didn't bother to prepare for whatever Judge Sanders had in store. Why would it matter anyway, especially if I just got tossed back in jail?

"Well, Judge Sanders, you said that you would have some other things for me to do after I got out."

"And I do, Lewis," he replied, opening a file on his desk. He asked bluntly, "Do you have the money to repay Mr. Krueger for his store front window?"

"No sir."

"I didn't think so. That's why I've set it up so you will be working for Mr. Krueger part time to help repay him for the window. It's the responsible thing to do."

My body tensed as the weight shifted in my feet. Judge Sanders was studying me. From the way he looked at me, he was pleased with my response. He continued.

"After you have worked sufficiently to pay the glass off you will be able to continue working for a full wage." He leaned forward in his chair and placed his elbows on the glass covering his desk, hands clasped. "That's of course if Mr. Krueger wants to keep you on. It could be the possibility of some steady work."

I wiped the perspiration from my forehead while Judge Sanders waited patiently. All sorts of possibilities played out in my head which made my desire for a drink even stronger. His proposal was nothing like what I had expected.

"I guess I'll do what I can Judge Sanders. I mean, I don't really have any experience working in a hardware store," I answered, trying to show interest.

"That's not a concern," he said brushing it off, "you'll pick up on it soon enough. It won't be anything too detailed, just helping Mr. Krueger with what he needs. Besides, like I said, it could be the possibility of full time employment if it works out. If I remember correctly you haven't had a steady job for a while now."

"I haven't had one since I left Mr. Pearson's auto garage in January. Since then I've just been getting steady work where I could," I answered, wanting to leave.

"You mean since you were fired," Judge Sanders corrected. I swallowed and nodded. He wasn't going to let anything go.

"What did you do before Mr. Pearson's?"

"Just odds and ends mostly, whatever was available and halfway steady to help support. Mr. Pearson's was the first steady job I had. I was there for roughly five years."

"Didn't you go to some college after you graduated high school? I thought you had headed off to . . ."

"I did, but that was a while ago and it didn't last very long," I said, trying to cut his probing off. I tried to get back on the subject, "When will I start work at Mr. Krueger's?"

"You will start tomorrow Lewis. The best thing for you is to stay busy and not have too much time on your hands while out in the community." He stood up and walked to the side of his desk, closer to me, and then his demeanor changed. "Is it all right with you if I share a bit of advice, from someone who used to hide in the bottle?"

I stared, mouth gaped slightly. Inside my chest the blood started pumping faster; I could feel it in my fingers. My mind was completely blank with surprise.

Judge Sanders had a sly grin on his face and was patient, waiting to see if I would come up with any response. I didn't.

"Have you reached the point where you have come to the understanding that you have a problem Lewis?" he asked, with a tone that was more like a friend than a judge. I still couldn't answer. I just stood there and looked at him, waiting for my vocal chords to process a response.

"It took me almost six years to realize that I had ruined my life and lost my family." He shook his head in disbelief. "I went on for *six years*. Hard to imagine that someone can fool themselves for that long." He looked away from me and out the window as his demeanor became increasingly somber. There was silence. Neither of us spoke for what seemed like an eternity.

As I came back to my senses I asked quietly, "You had a problem with . . . ?"

He laughed out loud. "Problem? Not exactly. More like an obsession."

I felt awkward and out of place, but I couldn't help but be intrigued. Why would he take the time to tell me this? I had known plenty of guys who were drunks, but they were *still* drunks. My mind began to search for someone—anyone—that I knew who that had been a drunk and then went dry. There wasn't a single one.

As he spoke, my eyes came to rest on his face. He was staring off at the wall on the opposite side of the room. "I was a wash out, slobbering fool of an alcoholic. Roaming from job to job. Does that sound familiar?"

A sense of shame washed over me, but I couldn't take my eyes off him, still completely surprised at what I was hearing. He walked over to the mantle that hovered over the fireplace. Framed pictures and various ornaments were carefully spread out.

"How did you get like that?" I asked.

"Well, how did *you* get like *this*?" he said, turning it back on me.

My soul was restless with anticipation. It had been so long since I had opened up to anyone. I had been so self-centered and irresponsible, the last thing I wanted to do was face someone about it. But, when Judge Sanders approached me as an outsider, seeming truly interested in understanding me, it was an opportunity I hadn't ever realized I needed. It was the first time I had ever *wanted* to talk to anybody about it.

I sat down and exhaled. I couldn't believe what I was about to do, but at the moment it felt right. "After watching my father slave away at the factory for twenty years, I vowed that after high school I would do something I enjoyed. So I worked hard and with my parents help I was able to go to college."

Feelings that had been locked away for years were trying to come out with my words. It was all I could do to hold them back. "I wanted to be an electrical technician and work on designing machines and prototypes and things of that nature. I used to love working with electronics and figuring how things functioned.

"I met Sadie my first year at school. She's from the southern part of the state, a small rural town. It was her first real stay in the city; she was scared to death. We hit it off and started dating. I brought her home that next summer to meet mom and dad and they formed a good relationship. We had it all planned out; I still had two years to go for my certification and she had one more in order to be able to teach. We would get married, have a family, and move back here. I would get a good job and when the kids were old enough she would teach and it would all work out." I finished, having formed a smile on my face—something I hadn't done for a quite a while.

"And what happened?" Judge Sanders asked softly.

"Sadie got pregnant halfway through our second year together. We should have known better, but we figured we were safe. I wanted to do what was right and we already knew we loved each other, but instead of only working part time and going to school, I had to start working full time. We got married and tried to save some money. My father had been renting out my old grandparents house and said that we could have it if we just paid a simple rent to him. It seemed like the only option," I explained, the smile slowly leaving. I couldn't stop talking.

"After working some odd jobs I finally got on at the garage. Mom watched Danielle while Sadie worked as a maid to help bring in income. To be perfectly honest, our life wasn't that bad and we had what we needed. But . . . but somewhere in the back of my mind I couldn't help but think I had been cheated out of something better. I didn't blame Sadie or Danielle—they mean everything to me. I just . . . there was more I could do, but I wasn't able to do it." I paused to steady my breath.

"Until last year; that's when things started picking up at the factory again and they had some openings come up. Everybody was trying to get on."

"I remember," he interjected.

"It wasn't what I wanted to do, but my thoughts about it had changed over the years seeing how much more I could make and how good the benefits were. Dad had worked up the ladder enough that he figured he could get me on. I actually met Mr. Masterson, dad's foreman, over at an open house. I probably had a pretty good chance, especially with dad working there, then . . . ," I stopped.

"So when your dad died in December, everything just kind of fell apart?"

I took another deep breath and thought hard about his question before answering. When I raised my head to answer him, I started to cry, but quickly brushed it away and continued. "It didn't seem fair. It all just went away. One minute things were looking up and then it completely fell out from under me.

"Pressure was building up and I didn't know what to do. He was the only one I felt I could talk to; I could always talk to him. It wasn't right to burden Sadie with my frustrations and my mother didn't really listen. He would listen and help me remember that I had to do what I had to do for my family. They came first, not me. It wasn't about what I needed; it was about what was best for the family . . . that's what he would tell me."

I wiped my forearm across my eyes. Judge Sanders didn't move, he was just listening. "I guess I just couldn't handle it. I drank periodically, just every now and then if we went out, but about two weeks after the funeral, I . . . I'm not even sure how I got so low, so far down, but I actually thought about . . . I . . ."

He paused briefly to see if I would continue. When I didn't, he said, "So it wasn't just your father dying; there were a lot of things building up to that?"

"It seems that way," I answered, not sure myself. "I had been at my mom's trying to get things finalized with his death and on the way home I started thinking and couldn't handle it. I stopped to get a drink. And then I had another, and another, and another . . .

My hands started to shake. I rubbed them together forcefully and continued. "I guess Sadie thought I was just getting over the death, which is why she wasn't as concerned, at first, as maybe she should have been. All I could remember the next day was it made all my thoughts go away about dad, about work, about college, and everything else. So when the thoughts and feelings came back again, it seemed like the logical answer. Over time, I guess I just let it take control."

Still standing by the mantle, he looked at me and asked, "And if I told you that the reason I started drinking caused me to feel all the same feelings, would you believe me?"

"I guess I would have to."

"My reason involved my father, but it was a little different. He would beat up on my mother and me. He was an angry man and when I got old enough, instead of confronting him about it, I ran away from it. I hid inside a bottle for almost six years before I came out. Never thought I would be able to overcome it. Never even thought I would want to; much less get through law school and become a judge and be sitting here having this conversation with you.

"Do you know what saved me?" There was no pause for a reply as he took one of the pictures off the mantle in his hand and answered, "A good, faithful woman, Lewis." The picture was of his wife, him, and their three children. He turned and spoke, but it wasn't as a judge, "Lewis, if you don't do something about your life now, you will spend the rest of your life regretting it. I can't force you to do anything and I can't just let you walk away without consequences."

Again, I didn't know what to say. I just sat there, taking it all in. He continued. "Do you want to stop drinking Lewis?"

"I don't know, Judge Sanders. To be honest, the first thing I was going to do after leaving your office was go get a drink. Is it enough to just want to stop?" I asked.

He made his way over to his desk and sat back down. "No, but that's pretty much the first step. I don't know what the sure fire way is. I guess there has to be some type of incentive, some reason that's strong enough. Is there any reason you can think of, right now talking to me, as to why you should change?"

Without hesitation I replied, "My daughter, Danielle."

Judge Sanders nodded gently. "How long have you been drinking heavy?"

"I guess about five months or so, well, six actually, since I've been locked up for this last month; though this last month has been the lightest month by far."

He leaned forward in his chair. "I'm no counselor Lewis, and I don't claim to be. The final decision comes to you. By the grace of God I was able to stop after six years. I would wager if you really wanted to, you could stop after six months."

"What do I do?" I asked, almost pleading. He made it sound so simple.

"I'm not exactly sure I have the answer to that, but I think I know what you *don't* do. You don't go to bars, you don't hang out with old friends who drink, and you don't just sit around doing nothing. This is why I've got something else for you to do other than working at Mr. Krueger's."

In all of the openness and admission I had completely forgot that he mentioned working at Krueger's. The reality of my situation started to set in again.

"You will work at Krueger's from two until six during the week and then on Saturday you will work from ten in the morning until five in the afternoon. Hopefully that will keep you fairly occupied; but just to make sure, I have something for you to do to keep you from sitting around in the morning. Do you know where St. Joseph's is?" he asked.

"The orphanage? I think so," I said.

"It's off of Main Street, down Franklin. The old Catholic church. Ring any bells?"

"I know where you're talking about."

"It's an orphanage. You will have to report there tomorrow to help them serve lunch to the children. You'll be there from eleven until about one-thirty everyday except for Saturdays. That includes helping on Sundays as well. It will be a good experience for you. Ms. Weston owes me one and I told her you would be a gracious, diligent volunteer. You will help out there for a month as part of your service to the community. Are you able to do that?"

18

My mind started racing again and I didn't answer. It would be simple. All I needed to do was go back to my first plan and head over to the liquor store. My palms told me it was time to leave.

His demeanor changed and he was back to being a judge. "Lewis, I need to know right now if you are going to take this opportunity and straighten yourself out?"

I stared at my feet as the struggle continued to wage inside. I knew it was the right thing to do—the thing I needed to do—but was I willing to do it? Was I willing to fight myself?

Judge Sanders stood; his voice a little more stern as he continued, "Because Lewis if you're not, then I would rather put you away right now and let you dry out for another month, or a year, or however long it takes. It doesn't do you, me, or this community any good to let you back out if you are going to endanger yourself and others."

He leaned forward and rested his hands on the desk, waiting for a response. Finally, knowing I could be honest with him, I answered truthfully. "If I told you yes, Judge Sanders, I would be lying. Give me two weeks to figure this all out, get straight with this work with Mr. Krueger and with helping out at the orphanage. If I don't think I'll be able to do it, I'll gladly walk over to the jail myself and close the door behind me."

He studied me as he sat back down. "For now, I guess I can accept that answer. Do I have your word?"

I didn't think it personally meant much, but instead of not caring, I was at least willing to try. Judge Sander's food for thought had given me something to munch on. "Yes, you have my word."

Completely overwhelmed and well past uncomfortable, I asked, "Is there anything else?"

"I would appreciate it if you keep what we talked about just between us. I'm not one to get involved where I don't belong, but I felt the need to step in. You've got some avenues now to help get your footing straight and I hope you take advantage of them."

"Thanks Judge Sanders. I won't tell anybody."

He nodded. "Report to the orphanage by eleven in the morning so Ms. Weston can give you a tour and introduce you to the kitchen staff. Then you will have to make your way down Main Street over to the hardware store. Mr. Krueger is expecting you at two." He wrote something on a piece of paper and handed it to me.

"Give this to Betty at the front desk. She'll give you a bus slip that allows you transportation on any of the city buses for a month. That should help you get on your feet. I already checked and there is a bus that runs from Main and Franklin down to Elm, right down the street from Krueger's. If that doesn't work, you'll have to talk it over with him."

"Yes Judge Sanders," I said, taking the paper. I turned and started for the door. But he spoke up.

"Lewis," he said before I opened the door. I turned back toward him. "If you *are* able to get yourself straight you would be a fool not to try and get your wife back."

I did not respond, but nodded and closed the door behind me, knowing he was right. But I knew I had no chance of getting Sadie back unless I could prove to her that I had changed.

And there was only one reason I had any desire to stay on the path to change. Only one reason that finally swayed me *not* to go on my first day out of jail and get wasted.

She was the only chance I had.

4

Still a Reason

"It's dad! Dad's here!" Danielle yelled at the top of her lungs when she saw me walking up the drive. My mother's house was not large, not by any sense of the word, but it was enough. An old one story, it was situated at the end of a long gravel drive, surrounded by a spacious yard and lots of trees.

She ran as fast as she could past the old Ford sedan that was parked at the end of the drive. The same car that a month ago had to be removed from Mr. Krueger's window. From what I could tell it had been fixed.

Danielle looked liked she had aged years since I last saw her. When she got close I knelt down. Her seven-year-old frame leapt into my arms.

"Are you going to come back and stay with us now?" There was no response. I just held her close, smelt her hair, and felt her cheek against mine. Holding her in the shade I realized that she was the only thing I had left. The only one who didn't judge. The only one in the innocence of youth who still loved me unconditionally, just because. I didn't want to break her heart just yet.

"We'll have to see baby. Did you miss me?" I said, extending my arms out so I could see her. She looked just like her mother; dark hair, crystal clear eyes, full cheeks, and a wonderfully wide smile.

"Yes I did, but you were gone for a long time this time." Danielle was very mature for her age. One thing Sadie never did was hide anything from her. Right or wrong, Danielle knew pretty much everything that was going on.

"I know. Dad messed up pretty bad this last time, huh?"

She nodded.

"Did mom tell you what happened?"

She nodded again. I nodded back. The wind blew and we both turned our heads toward a long, rattling station wagon as it passed. She grabbed my finger.

"Are you going to do it again?" she asked sincerely, seriously, her eyes gently pleading.

"I'm working on it sweetie," was all I could muster.

My head jerked toward the porch as the front door squeaked and my mother stepped out. After all these years, she still looked the same as she did when I was a child. Her apron tightly tied around her healthy frame, ruffles along the top and the tying strings soiled and stained. Her light eyes peering through her only pair of spectacles that she had miraculously been able to maintain since what seemed like my birth. A dark dress, firm hands, and those awful black semi-heeled shoes. She claimed they went with everything. I thought they just made her look older and heavier.

I stood to be polite, waved, and raised my voice so she could hear me. "Hi mama."

She routinely waved back and made her way over to one of the two rocking chairs my father had built. I picked up Danielle and made my way to the porch.

When I got to the steps I put Danielle down, walked over, and kissed mama on the head.

"It's good to see you," I said softly and sat down in the vacant chair. It got quiet. The crickets in the back woods and the cars periodically humming past on Thurman Street were the only sounds that could be heard in the silence.

I glanced over at my mother and saw her staring out over the yard, contemplating. Danielle looked at me, smiled, and moved towards the door.

I nodded and she slowly got up and made her way into the house without looking at either of us. After a few seconds I heard the back door screen slam shut. Confrontation was something my daughter avoided at all cost. She was getting as far away from us as she could.

Mom started. "I'm glad that you at least came over sober." It wasn't much, but it was more positive than I was expecting. And it was true, I was sober.

"I really wanted to see you and Danielle. A month is a long time."

"It sure is." She continued to stare out as clouds slowly rolled to the east, toward the coast.

"Thanks for letting them stay with you."

"That's no problem. There's room enough. I wish the circumstances were different, but there's nothing I can do about that."

There was nothing she could do and I wasn't going to get upset at the comment. I didn't feel like fighting. I had to thank my mother and apologize to her at the same time. If she wanted to give me a sermon, that was her choice. I was going to keep it short and to the point.

"I start a new job tomorrow."

I thought that might break her concentration. She didn't lose the rhythm in her chair. With all she had recently been through, I think her stubbornness was the one thing that helped her stay sane.

"I'm going to be with Mr. Krueger, over at the hardware store. At first, I'll work to help pay off the window, but Judge Sanders said if I work well I can stay on full time. Mr. Krueger needs some extra help."

"Well I hope that works out," she said, keeping her straightforward glance.

There was another pause of silence. Mr. Henderson was coming down the road with the mail. We both waved in unison as he opened my mom's box and put in a few letters. He waved back and continued his quick pace down the street.

"How often are you going to come by?" she asked.

"A couple of times a week I guess, to see Danielle. I'm also volunteering at St. Joseph's orphanage for lunch. So with that and work the only time I can come over is in the morning. I mean . . . if that's all right."

Again, she nodded. There was something else she wanted to say, but she didn't.

"For what it's worth, I'm really going to try and stop this time. And I promise I won't come around if I drink any."

There was no response, but the look on her face told me that she wasn't sure I could do it. I couldn't blame her.

"Do you need anything?" she asked in an unusually motherly fashion, taking me by surprise.

"I don't think so. Sadie said there's stuff at the house for me."

Her eyes started to well and she took a breath. I could see the hurt, the pleading. She turned and finally looked at me. "I really do love you Lewis," she said softly. "I hope you know that."

Danielle came walking around the house before she had the chance to say anything else. I gently rose, walked over, and kissed my mother on her head again. Wiping my eyes quickly I responded, "I know mama. I know."

A few tears fell down her cheek. I made my way down the steps and walked with Danielle to the end of the drive. I wiped my eyes discretely so Danielle wouldn't see.

"Thanks for giving us some time alone, Danielle."

"Is she mad at you?"

"I guess so, but she has a right to be mad at me."

"Daddy?" I smiled as she took hold of my hand. "I'm not mad at you." She paused, and looked directly in my eyes, "but I hope that this time things can go back to how they were before grandpa died."

All I could do was hug her and choke the feelings coming up inside.

"Me too, sweetie." I wiped my eyes again and tried to smile. "Can I come and see you in a couple of days?"

She nodded.

I kissed her on the cheek and walked back down the drive. Even though the pain of my daughter's words rang in my ear, it was the time with my mother that weighed on my mind as I made my way to the bus stop. There was a different emotion. No yelling or pointing fingers, at least not out right. And she told me that she loved me. Deep down I knew she did, that's what mothers are supposed to do, but it was nice to hear.

But instead of finding happiness in the moment, I knew that the pain that came with my mother's tears was from me. Just like Sadie's tears, I knew I was to blame. The guilt inside of me built as I made my way down Thurman Street toward the bus stop.

❖   ❖   ❖

When I reached the front door, there was a part of me hoping it would be locked and the key wouldn't work so I could have an excuse to go get a drink.

No such luck. The key worked just fine. I turned around toward the front yard again, waiting for Danielle to come down the street from a friend's house, or Sadie to pull in from work. Wishful thinking. Actually, it was detrimental thinking. The last thing I needed was false hope. Reality is what I needed and when the front door squeaked open I had all the reality I needed solemnly staring back at me.

Empty furniture in the living room to the right, an odorless kitchen through the opening straight ahead, a dark dining room off the back right corner, and the hallway to the left that contained two small bedrooms and a bathroom.

I put my keys in their usual place on the fire mantle next to the door. The room was dim and almost colorless. As I stood there, the afternoon sun blazing through the sheer curtains, I began to realize how much in my life had been taken for granted. I had missed six months of my family's life; six months I wouldn't be able to get back.

The few groceries Sadie left were positioned neatly on the kitchen shelf. I made my way to an empty chair at the dining room table and slowly sat down to look out the window in the living room. It was a beautiful, cloudless day, but it was hard to tell with all the shadows spread over the walls.

On top of the table was the tablecloth that Sadie had made. It felt soft and shiny underneath my fingertips. I repositioned the lopsided cloth and relaxed in the chair, mind completely empty, not knowing where to start.

A cross with Jesus strewn about it rested on a nail on the wall above the table. The small china cabinet in the corner was empty. Under the table was an area rug my mother and father had received for their wedding. The rug had probably not moved an inch in ten years.

I got up and walked into the kitchen. On the counter there was some tuna fish, canned meat, bread, bananas, cantaloupe, and tomatoes. Sadie never wanted to see me again, but she had still brought me some groceries. It didn't make any sense.

As I licked my lips with thirst, I realized how wet I was with sweat. The house had been locked up tight as a drum. I made my way through the house and lifted every window I could to help circulate the air.

When I walked back into the kitchen I passed the fridge, and stopped. Even with the few sips from Moses every so often, it had been about five days since my last drink. Nothing would have tasted better in the world than a cold beer, right out of the fridge. Just the thought made my hand shake and my mouth water more feverishly.

Without thought I opened the fridge to discover a pitcher of water and some mayonnaise, mustard, and ketchup. There was nothing *real* to drink. I was all alone. Nobody was there with me. My wife had given up on me. My daughter couldn't be with me. The pain began to build.

I reached for the pitcher of water and started to swallow, but it didn't quench my hurt or my thirst. I slung it across the kitchen with a loud scream. The pots on the oven crashed to the ground and rolled to a stop on the sopping floor. When I slammed the fridge door shut, the few plates and glasses on top of it clamored to the floor and broke in what seemed like a million pieces.

Swinging. Crying. Yelling. Aching. I punched the side of the fridge once, twice; then with the third I felt a pain in my right hand. The sweat and tears in my eyes made it hard to see as I fell to the floor, leaning against the fridge sobbing like a devastated child.

There were no thoughts involved, just emotion: pain and anger, guilt and hopelessness. I didn't stop it; I couldn't stop it. I sat there, huddled, for about five minutes; oblivious to anything and everything around me as the pain inside dripped out of my eyes, nose, and mouth onto my shirt.

Eventually, when the episode passed and silence once again came over me, I gently raised myself up and made it into the bathroom. I carefully took off my damp shirt and winced at the throbbing in my right hand, soaked a towel in the cool faucet water, and wiped my face. My eyes were puffy and swollen, and my cheeks were blushed, drenched in sweat. My grip on the towel tightened and I rammed my left hand into the disgrace looking back at me.

Surprisingly it didn't hurt. The glass cracked, but did not shatter, and I felt somewhat calmer. It was a step. I was disgusted with myself.

I got to bed, fell into it, and closed my eyes. The day was done. I had made it through one day of freedom.

5

Responsibility

Directly inside the front gate of St. Joseph's, rows of apple trees were in bloom down the wide gravel drive that circled up to the main entrance. A stone wall around the property made the orphanage feel like a city unto itself.

Built around the turn of the century, the main building was a large, brick chapel with stained glass windows. There were more modern extensions that flanked the sides. The addition to the right was single story while the extension to the left had two levels.

When I reached the front steps, my brain became conscious of the still steady pulsing in my bruised hand. Thankfully it didn't seem to be broken.

The only way I found the energy to get out of bed that morning and actually catch the bus was by taking a long, cold bath. I don't know why, but I purposefully ignored my distorted reflection in the bathroom mirror. Deep down I really wanted to hit it again.

The kitchen was still a mess. I couldn't find the strength or will to clean it up. With all the doubts and uncertainty spinning around inside, the comfort of my own bed outweighed them all—at least for the night. When I finally woke around 9:00am, well rested and sober, I was willing to give Judge Sander's experiment a try.

It was a gorgeous day outside and the short walk from Main to St. Joseph's helped me clear my mind some. Before I even had time to knock on the solid double doors, a stout young nun, wearing glasses and holding a notepad came out. Her robes snugly fit her large frame. She seemed eager.

"Are you Mr.", she hesitated to check her notes, "Anderson?"

"Yes ma'am, I'm here to help with lunch."

"I am Sister Maria. Follow me please. Ms. Weston is waiting."

Inside, the main lobby was small, but the large vaulted ceiling seemed to add space. Instead of continuing through the two doors directly in front of me, or heading through the door on the left, I followed Sister Maria to the right through an opening that led to a more modern hallway.

The corridor was lined with doors and offices. As I looked in each one, sisters were going about their various responsibilities. We passed the sanitation, nurses, and education offices before reaching the end of the hall and the sign over the door that read 'Administrators Office'. At the back of the room were three large, clear windowpanes. With the office door open, it was the only source of natural light along the hallway. The playground area in the back of the grounds was in full view through the window. I could see no children, only vacant seesaws, slides, and a sand pit.

The office consisted of an old, wooden secretary's desk on the left, four chairs lining the back wall, and a door to the right that was closed. Along the door's glass was painted 'Ms. Weston, Head Administrator.' All of the furnishings in the office looked well used, but it was clean and tidy.

Sister Maria took her place behind the desk and placed her notebook next to a typewriter. "Ms. Weston will see you in a minute Mr. Anderson. You can have a seat," she said, gesturing to the chairs on the back wall.

I sat down and Sister Maria started banging away on the typewriter. Shortly thereafter Ms. Weston walked out of her office.

"You must be Mr. Anderson," asked a trim woman wearing a dark dress and rimmed glasses with her light brown hair pulled up in a bun.

"Yes ma'am," I said, standing. She seemed out of place among all the sisters.

"Oh please, call me Ms. Weston. There are no ma'am's around here, only the sisters and me," she said pleasantly. "Please step into my office—and please, take any messages for me Sister Maria." Sister Maria nodded, staying focused on whatever she had begun to type.

I followed her into her scant office, quite cluttered, with only a small desk, a few filing cabinets and two chairs for visitors. Just like the waiting room, there was a direct view to the playground through the window behind her desk.

"Please have a seat Mr. Anderson," she asked kindly and sat down herself. "I was glad to hear that somebody could come in and help us out. I know Sister Catherine has been pulling her hair out. Have you ever worked in a cafeteria setting before?"

"Uh, no ma'am. I mean, no, Ms. Weston," I stumbled, remembering her request, "unfortunately I haven't."

It didn't seem to discourage her any. "Well, it's not detrimental. Sister Catherine is an old pro and can get you into the swing of things. I'm interested in someone who can be on time, put in a good effort while they're here, and get along with the children. Does that sound reasonable to you?"

"Yes. I guess so," I answered, repositioning myself in the chair.

"I was so excited when Judge Sanders called and said he knew a friend who was looking for an opportunity to keep him busy. You must know him pretty well; he sure did put in a good word for you."

31

There was a sudden feeling in my chest that made me pause. She didn't know. She thought I was there of my own free will.

"He did?"

"Yes he did and so I was glad to meet with you. Sister Catherine can be a bit demanding, but it's only for a few hours a day and you'll have a hot lunch waiting for you before you go. And having a positive, male role model for the children will be an added blessing. So can you help us out?" She waited for my response, still holding an agreeable smile.

"Yes." No other words came. A friend of Judge Sanders? A positive role model? My hands started to itch a little.

Ms. Weston continued smiling. "Well then, that's wonderful. Would you like me to show you to the lunch room now?" she asked as she stood.

"Uh . . . okay," I replied standing, putting my hands in my pockets. She left brief instructions with Sister Maria and hurried out of the office with a gesture for me to follow.

"Lunch is at 12:00pm sharp, so they've already started preparing, but you should be able to give some assistance today. And remember what I said about Sister Catherine; she's old and a little bossy, but don't let her get to you."

I nodded in response, but she was already ahead of me, quickening her pace as she made her way down the hall toward the front entrance.

"You are just going to love it here. I've been here about three years and couldn't wish for a better place to work," she said as we reached the main foyer.

"The church hired me to come and run things about three years ago when their numbers started increasing. My background is with juvenile detention, so needless to say," she said swinging open the door to the chapel, "this was a wonderful change of pace."

"How many children are here?" I asked as we made our way to the front of the chapel and took a left toward a side door.

"Approximately forty-five children from infants to the age of fourteen. It fluctuates from time to time, but it usually stays around that range"

She opened the door and stepped into a small foyer. "This door to the left leads to the first floor hallway, which contains the boys sleeping quarters. This set of stairs goes up to the second floor where the girls reside. This door at the back goes through the education rooms and on to the cafeteria."

She opened the door and led me into another small foyer. Six wooden doors were placed between the very brightly painted white walls.

"Here are where the students have class. We have five wonderful sisters who teach the different age groups. They are in class from nine to noon and then they head through this door for lunch," she said, pointing to the door with the cafeteria sign on it. "Then there is nap time for the younger children and play time for the older. Then at three they go back to classes until five; then they wash up for dinner at five-thirty, then they have chores, then free time, then prayers, and then it's time for bed."

I tried to keep up with her schedule, but as soon as the door to the kitchen was open, there stood an elderly woman with ladle in hand. She was pointing it directly at me.

"Is this the one, Ms. Weston?" she asked. Ms. Weston nodded and the woman made her way towards us. The kitchen area was modest and surprisingly modernized. Two other workers, both women, were running back and forth as she walked towards me. She looked like death with a hair net. Rigid, very thin, almost sickly looking—it was Sister Catherine.

She grabbed one of the aprons off the refrigerator and shoved it in my direction. "Put this on, grab that pot, take the broccoli," she demanded, pointing to a clump of freshly bought, unwrapped vegetables on the table, "and get to boiling." She turned and walked away.

"Welcome to the kitchen," Ms. Weston said, somewhat sarcastically. "You better do what she says. If you need anything, I'll more than likely be in my office."

I worked in the kitchen and followed orders. Without thought, I did whatever Sister Catherine asked and kept my mouth closed. She didn't want me serving on my first day so I stayed in the back. When it came time to serve, I could only hear the footsteps of what seemed like a thousand kids coming through the lunch line. I was perfectly happy just dealing with the broccoli.

Ms. Weston stopped by the cafeteria again before I left and thanked me for helping. When the time came to go I was so anxious to leave that I skipped the free lunch, quickly exited out the back, and made my way to the bus stop. With the thought of facing Mr. Krueger, I wasn't really hungry anyway.

❖   ❖   ❖

The bell above the door rang out in a loud, clattered chorus, but nobody in the store seemed to pay it any mind. I turned to close the door and my heart dropped as I saw the brand new window pane to the left. It seemed like it happened so long ago that it wasn't even real anymore.

Mr. Krueger's store took up about twenty-five feet of frontage space along Main Street. A small register sat in the front of the store on the right with two middle aisles that ran down the center with shelves on each of the sidewalls. It was crowded, but clean, with small signs hanging from the center to give shoppers some idea of what direction to go. All the way at the back was a small curtained opening with a sign reading 'Storage' above it.

The curtain opened and Mr. Krueger walked out. He was an older, portly man, balding with curly hair on the sides and a bushy moustache. From all that I ever heard about him, he was even keeled; kind when he had to be and stern when needed, but always fair. He was walking my way.

"Mr. Krueger," I said with a lump in my throat.

"Yes sir. How may I help you?" he asked politely, not recognizing me.

"Uh, Mr. Krueger, my name is Lewis Anderson. Judge Sanders said he talked to you," I said, nervous.

Surprisingly, his demeanour did not change. "Oh yes, Mr. Anderson. Judge Sanders did talk with me. Is this situation that we worked out going to be okay with you?" he asked bluntly.

"Um . . . yes sir, if it's okay with you," I answered, rubbing my hands together, still not sure what I was getting myself into.

"Come this way then." He led me to the back of the store and through the curtain. In the back was a storeroom, the same width but much smaller in length than the rest of the store, with various boxes and crates scattered around the floor. To the right were two small doors; one of them had a hook on it with some aprons. Scrunched in the back right corner was a small accounting desk.

"The door over there with the aprons is the bathroom. The one next to it is a closet that has the cleaning supplies: broom, mop, bucket and the like. Everything else is pretty straightforward. Do you know how to read?" he asked simply.

"Yes sir."

"Good. It will be pretty simple. Your main duties are to keep the floors clean, as well as the bathroom. Then when the bins or shelves get low on an item, you just come back here, find it, and then restock. Once a week, every Thursday, we get shipments in. So every Wednesday a big job will be to make sure this back area is clean and tidy. Take your time to make sure you know where all the supplies are now; that way when the truck comes you'll know where to put them. Everything okay so far?"

I nodded, overwhelmed.

"The only thing I ask is that you are polite to the customers and that you don't touch the register. You're not a sales clerk, but if a customer asks you a question and you know where something is, well then feel free to answer them. Otherwise, be sure to send them to me." He looked me in the eyes for the first time, paused for a moment, and continued, his voice slightly softer.

"I've got nothing against you personally, Mr. Anderson. If you don't make a big deal about it, neither will I. I appreciate you coming to work off your debt to me and as long as you give me reason to trust you, I will. If you have any questions, please ask. To start off, why don't you sweep up the front of the store?"

"Yes sir, Mr. Krueger." I didn't know what else to say. It didn't seem like he wanted me to say anything. He wanted me to do the job. No more, no less. It wasn't a necessarily friendly reception. It wasn't a harsh one either, so I wasn't going to complain.

He walked back out to the front and I made my way over to the closet. I put on an apron, found the broom and started work.

The afternoon was easy enough and my nerves subsided as I became more comfortable with the surroundings. I swept, stocked, and tried to stay out of the way. Nothing very demanding. It took a while to get used to the ringing of the bell as customers came in and out periodically. The most involvement I had with anybody during the day was saying 'excuse me' to customers.

Mr. Krueger didn't bother me and I didn't bother him unless I had to. At the end of day he thanked me, signed off a little card he had made as a reminder of how much I still had to work off, and shook my hand before I left.

As the bell rang behind me an unexpected feeling of ease swept over me. Mr. Krueger was seeing me eye to eye and trusting me even though he had every reason not to. The man's front window had been smashed to bits. Somebody could have been seriously hurt, or even killed. Yet, he treated me like I was a new employee showing up for the first day of work. It's not that I didn't appreciate his generosity—it was just hard to understand.

I realized walking to the bus stop that I had an opportunity to prove myself. An opportunity to show someone with an open mind that I could be responsible; that I was capable. There were no prejudices or preconceived notions.

Mr. Krueger was giving me a shot. I didn't get my hopes up, but I was willing to give it at least one more day.

6

The Girl

"Daddy!"

Danielle was on the front porch playing with the next-door neighbor's cat, Sparky. That morning I needed something to lift me up and a cold bath didn't sound as therapeutic as it did the day before. I had to see Danielle again.

When she yelled out to me the cat scattered, running off the side of the porch and into the trees.

"How's Sparky doing?" I asked as I reached the porch and stretched out my arms for a hug.

"Good," Danielle said, wrapping her arms around my neck. "I think she likes it better over here because Ms. Thompson isn't very nice to her."

She pulled back to look at me directly. "Why would somebody want to keep a cat if they aren't going to be nice to it? Why get it in the first place?"

"I don't think people do it on purpose. It's just something that happens after they've been around each other too long.

They just kind of like to . . . just think of it as they like to take breaks from each other."

"Kind of like you and mom are taking a break?" she asked sincerely.

"I guess, maybe kind of like that sweetie."

"Do you think you and mom will fall in love again?" she asked. There was no pleading. It was a sincere question that showed a desire to want to understand, to know what to expect and have no surprises.

I still loved Sadie and deep down I thought she still loved me. It didn't seem like it had anything to do with love—it had to do with commitment. But I didn't want to confuse Danielle. "Do you mean will we get back together?"

She nodded.

"I don't know baby. I'm going to try. Do you understand why she doesn't want to be with me right now?"

Again, she nodded. Even if she didn't fully understand, I knew she understood enough. That was all I wanted her to understand at the moment.

My mother was in the kitchen and I could hear the sporadic noise of pans being shuffled. She was cleaning up from breakfast.

"How is it with Grandma?" I asked, trying to change the subject.

"I guess its okay. It would be nice to have my own room again instead of sleeping with mom, but there's a lot to do and there are some other kids I can play with that are my age. Grandma's helping me read better too, so that's good."

"That's nice of grandma. Does mom . . ."

My mother appeared in the frame of the front screen. "Danielle, I need your help in the kitchen, please," she said.

"Hi mama," I replied. She nodded and turned around to head back toward the kitchen.

She bent down and wrapped her arms around me. "I love you, daddy"

"I love you too sweetie. You better get inside."

❖   ❖   ❖

40

Luke warm hamburgers and diced potatoes were not my idea of a great lunch, but it was free. I found a table in the dining area near the back exit away from the children and commenced the consumption of my reward for a few hours work. Margaret and Mary Beth, the other two helpers in the kitchen, had made their way out back to enjoy the nice weather at one of the picnic tables. I didn't really feel like being social.

Being around so many kids made me nervous, even though they were well behaved. There was a feeling of being out of place. At least that was how I felt; even though the kids didn't offer me a second glance as I helped to serve lunch.

For the most part the sisters were friendly, but stern, so the kids seemed to know how they were supposed to act. They came in and orderly got their trays, utensils, and food, and then sat down to eat.

One of the biggest surprises for me was the emotional tone that surrounded the orphanage. In an environment I assumed would be surrounded with sorrow and opposition there was laughter and happiness. Whatever the sisters were doing, they were doing it well. The children had no family, no real place to call home—and yet there was a warm, comfortable feeling.

At least everyone seemed warm and comfortable, with the exception of Sister Catherine. As I looked up from my table into the open door of the kitchen I could see white streams of smoke coming in from the window. I wasn't sure if sisters were supposed to smoke; but even if they weren't, I couldn't imagine anybody telling Sister Catherine to put it out. I took another bite of my hamburger and glanced around at some of the kids.

Ms. Weston said that as the children got older the chance of them being adopted decreased. People wanted to adopt smaller children that were still cuddly, not school age children who could have already grown into a 'bad seed.' After they turned sixteen most of the kids were set up with jobs and let out on their own. Ms. Weston said that one of the saddest things about working at the orphanage was rarely ever hearing from any of the older kids who had left.

"Would you like something to drink, mister?"

The shock of the sudden figure appearing to my right nearly caused me to choke on the beef. I held up my pointy finger, regained my composure and said, reluctantly, "Yes. Thank you very much."

Her black, curly, messy hair bounced as she made her way over to the food line to get a glass and then over to the water fountain. On her way back, her faded yellow dress seemed to bring out the whites of her eyes against her dark face. Her once white, casual shoes were dirty and tight; somewhat misplaced against her dress. Stepping gently, but surely, she held my glass of water in one hand and an old, ruffed and handled light-brown teddy bear in the other. The bear looked almost silly in the hands of one beyond the years of such things. She looked to be about twelve years old.

"Here's your water." She made a conscious effort to place the glass steady on the table so it wouldn't tip over.

"Thank you very much." I waited for her to leave so I could try and somehow swallow my lunch in peace.

"Just thought I'd be nice," she said matter-of-factly. She continued to stand, waiting for something.

I looked around, took another bite of my hamburger, and hoped that she would leave. As I chewed, she stuck out her right hand, the left still clinging to the small teddy bear, and introduced herself in a very polite tone. "My name is Dee."

I finished my bite, wiped my hand on the napkin and extended my arm to return her politeness. "My name is Lewis. It's nice to meet you Dee."

"It's nice to meet you too, Lewis," she replied, smiling brightly. "You're new, huh?"

"Yeah. I'm going to be helping out for a little while."

"That's nice to know. It's always good to see new faces. Nothing against the ones here, but they get kind of old to look at sometimes." She leaned over a little and whispered, "Have you met Sister Catherine yet?"

A small laugh came out. Having only known Sister

Catherine for barely twenty-four hours, I could understand where Dee was coming from.

"But it's not that bad," she continued, still standing, clutching her bear. "The kids are mostly nice and the sisters are good people. They don't hit us or make us do lots of work. I think you'll like being here. Do you know how long you will be here for?" she asked.

"Uh, I'm not really sure," I answered, half-lying and trying with my tone to encourage her to leave.

"Most people stay for only a few months," she answered, confidently sitting down on the chair across the table from me. She looked extremely comfortable and didn't seem to care that I had not invited her to sit down.

She was a yappy little thing. She talked and I listened as my food became officially cold. As much as I didn't want company, her voice grew on me and she seemed so sincere, I would have felt bad to turn her away. It was hard not to look into her eyes; they were crystal clear.

A slight smile remained on my lips as she talked about the sisters, her schooling, friends, and overall life at the orphanage. Either she talked all the time or she was desperate for company. But even through her all her chatting there was a maturity about her.

"Did you already eat?" I was able to ask as she took a much needed pause to breathe.

"Yeah, I figure the faster I can get it down the better it will taste. And hamburgers are about the worst thing here," she added, pointing to my tray. "But don't worry, they only serve the same meal twice a month, so you won't have to suffer this bad for another couple of weeks. Well, that's if you're still here."

My head quickly turned toward the entrance as a loud ringing pierced the hall. The bell tower in the chapel tolled once. When the bell stopped, Dee stood up and asked, "Will you be here tomorrow?"

"As far as I know, I'll be here most days."

She smiled and turned to leave with her class. When she did, her teddy bear fell to the floor. I reached over and picked

43

it up, feeling the soft, smooth fur. There was a small velvet scarf around its neck and I could barely make out an upper-case 'D' written under one of the feet, but couldn't make out the other letters, which probably spelled out 'Dee'. As I handed the bear to her, I asked, "What is his name?"

"Reginald."

"Where did you get the name Reginald?"

"Oh, my dad came up with the name for him. I got him a few years ago for my birthday."

My spine tingled. It was easier to believe that each of the children had never known their parents; that they grew up as orphans. To think that they once had known their parents and now had to be without them was heartbreaking.

"Well, okay Lewis, so I'll probably see you tomorrow?"

"I'll be here," I replied and watched her make her way through the double doors, getting mixed in with the crowd of children heading to their respective classes.

I took my tray back to the kitchen area to get ready for cleanup. Sister Catherine gave me a piercing glance for what seemed like no reason. It was something I was going to have to get used to.

As I started washing the dishes I got lost in my thoughts and Danielle came to my mind. I thought about how much I loved her and how much I wanted to be there for her. Then my thoughts switched from Danielle to the kids at lunch. With what Dee had said about her father, I could not look at the kids as a group, as orphans. It struck me that they were each individuals, all from different circumstances. All of them, I imagined, would have given anything to have their parents back, or at least a loving family to accept them as their own. That's all that my daughter wanted.

By the time I got done with my thoughts—and the washrag—the dishes that day were probably the cleanest they had ever been.

7

The First Test

"Do you have any questions from yesterday Lewis?" Mr. Krueger asked as I walked through the door. He was standing at the register positioning a small display.

"No sir."

"You did a good job Lewis," he said walking toward the back. "As I mentioned before, Wednesday's are very important. We need to straighten up the back to get ready for new shipments.

"I would ask that as we work today that you pay close attention to what we are doing. It would be an extreme help if you were to eventually be able to prep the stock room by yourself." He stopped and looked at me to make sure I was paying attention.

I nodded. Judge Sanders had mentioned that if I proved myself, there may be a long term position possible. But that seemed so far down the road, I couldn't see that far. I knew I had to take everything—Krueger's', the orphanage, the situation with Sadie, not drinking—day by day.

He parted the curtain and we stepped into the stockroom. The room was more cluttered than the day before.

"At all costs this back room needs to be completely clear. There needs to be a path from the back door to the middle. Any items that can be stocked in the front, without making bins too full, put it where it goes in the front. If there is anything left, it needs to be stacked up against the sides of the wall. Does that make sense?" His thick moustache was straight on his lips as he looked at me for a response.

"So just restock what I can, put any trash where it goes, and then any leftovers up against the wall? Is that right?"

"That's all I ask," he answered, as if almost begging me to get it right. "And," he started, moving over to the small bookkeeping desk in the corner, "I almost forgot." He was walking backward and pointed behind him at the desk. When he did, he knocked over a small, oval picture frame that lay on the top most shelf. Turning around he placed the picture back in its place and then stood in front of it. "Please, whatever you do, don't worry about cleaning this desk off. I have a system for billing and accounts. This is the only thing that you don't need to worry about. You don't need to touch anything on here," he said with a strong urging.

"No problem Mr. Krueger. If I have any questions about anything I'll be sure to ask," I replied.

"Well then I'll let you get to work," he said and went back out to the front.

My curiosity got the better of me and I glanced at the picture that he had knocked over. It was a couple holding each other, both smiling wildly. A man that was undoubtedly a younger Mr. Krueger was on the left while a shorter, medium build, curly haired women stood on the right. They were standing in front of the store.

I looked over to see if Mr. Krueger was coming. I gently picked up the picture and turned it over. Written across the wooden back was:

'Henry and Margie – Store Opening'

I turned the picture over to look at her again. I got the sense that she was no longer alive, but I didn't know that for sure. Gently, I put the picture back on the shelf and went over to pick up my apron. There was a hint of guilt for invading Mr. Krueger's privacy.

The task of cleaning out the back room turned out to be a chore. There were boxes, small bags, and random items all over the place. Mr. Krueger didn't seem like an untidy type of man, especially with how clean and orderly the front stayed. With only himself to keep the store straight, it must have been a lot to juggle.

It was hot and humid, a little musty, and the more I moved stuff around the more the air got dusty. Moving, rearranging, throwing away, lifting, putting down and lifting again put me through quite a work out. When I was finished, every ounce of me seemed filthy. As the cool water from the bathroom sink hit my face, it was completely satisfying.

"That's not a bad job at all," Mr. Krueger said, rather surprised, as he walked through the curtain. He had not had a chance to come in and check on me because of the afternoon rush as people were heading home.

"So everything looks okay?" I asked trying to be humble, but feeling very proud. It had taken the good part of three hours to get everything straight. I didn't wait for him to reply again. "Once I get the hang of it, it will be a little smoother."

"But you did fine Lewis . . . you did just fine," he interjected, nodding. He continued, not letting me revel in my effort. "So tomorrow when the truck comes, just try and keep it organized. There's so much merchandise that comes in each week that there's no real place to put it. As long as we can get to it, everything will be okay."

By the time I had finished it was almost time for me to leave, so I quickly swept up the front and made sure everything was in order. I said goodbye to Mr. Krueger, filled out my time card, and walked out into the August air. The breeze wasn't as hot as it had been and it felt refreshing passing over my still sweaty neck and arms.

In trying to keep with Judge Sander's advice to stay busy, I had decided to walk home at night if the weather was nice, instead of taking the bus. After getting out of Mr. Krueger's at 6pm, taking about forty-five minutes to get home, then another hour or so to cook dinner and eat, there wasn't much time for me to do anything else but sleep. With an honest days work under my belt, the walk home almost felt like a reward, something I deserved.

Most of Main was closing down for the day, but there were still plenty of people around. Being in jail for a month helped me appreciate being out in the open and around others; to hear hushed talk and the passing of cars. Something about taking in the busyness of life that was sort of energizing.

Instead of heading straight on Main all the way down to Maple, I decided to hang a left onto Donovan and squinted as I walked into the slowly setting sun. I wanted to go past the courthouse in hopes of running into Judge Sanders. I wanted to be able to tell him that so far everything was going good. To have that affirmation would have been uplifting.

But I stopped and decided against it. What a stupid idea!

So I turned around and headed back to Main to take the more direct route home. As I entered back into the crowded street again, with people heading home from work or getting last minute shopping done, my thoughts turned to Danielle.

And then to Sadie.

First I felt doubt, then thinking over the last few days a little bit of hope, which formed into a non-committed 'we'll see' attitude. The same feelings I expressed with Judge Sanders. Really nothing had changed. A few days were a few days, but in reality they weren't anything. Not really to me, probably not to Judge Sanders—definitely not to Sadie. The walk home was long and lonely.

When I finally turned the corner onto my street I saw the front porch . . . and hesitated. There was somebody sitting on the porch smoking a cigarette.

It was Marcus.

My mind went blank and I started to turn around and walk back the way I came, but my feet were not fast enough.

"Lewis! Hey, Lewis!" he yelled down the block and got up and started walking toward me, throwing his cigarette butt into the street. I exhaled and started walking toward him, putting on my best face. He was the last person I had expected, or really wanted, to see.

"My man Lewis, I can't believe it," he said as he got closer and stuck out his hand for a half shake, half hug. "I heard that you got out and here you are."

"Yep, here I am!," I said with a half laugh. "What'cha up to Marcus? Seems like forever?" I replied, trying to act excited.

"You know, same ol'. Just trying to make it. Heard my main man was free and wanted to come catch up and celebrate and see what's what," he replied, not sure where to go next.

"That's real good man, I appreciate that. I ain't really seen anybody since I got out. So that's nice of you to stop by," I said, semi-sincerely. In all honesty, it's not that I didn't want to see him; it's just that it wasn't the right time. I wasn't ready. We started walking back to the house.

"I heard the judge got you doing all kinds of stuff," he continued. I started to explain what I was doing with the orphanage and with Krueger's as we made our way to the front porch. He listened and nodded. We had been high school friends, but lost touch after graduation. But, after dad died, the places I started hanging out made it almost inevitable that we would hook up again. Marcus unfortunately had a hard time keeping down a steady job and went back and forth from staying with his parents to whatever woman he had in his life.

By the time we reached the front porch, I could tell he was done with the small talk. "That's all good man. I'm glad you're out. Look, let's head out and celebrate man," he said, eyebrow raised with a grin on his face. "I mean you been locked up for a month and I ain't had nobody to spend time with or talk to about stuff and what's up with all my . . . *women*" he said, pausing for affect. I couldn't help but laugh.

"I bet," I replied, still laughing.

49

"You see, that's what I'm talking about. You need to get out and loosen up some. Let's head down to Olsen's and say hi to everybody, they would love to see you," he said, grabbing my arm gently and trying to nudge me off the porch. I started laughing again, not sure what to do.

The invitation was tempting—after he said it I could feel it in my mouth. I swallowed hard.

"I can't tonight man. I wish I could, but I can't," I replied. It was the only thing I could think to say.

He let go of my arm still grinning. "Oh come on man, what do you mean 'you can't'. You're not locked up. You're off of work. I mean shoot, your old lady ain't even around to say nothing about it. Looks to me like it's the best time you can," he replied, still smiling, and waited for a response.

Something hit me in the pit of my stomach and my expression sank. Trying not to be rude, but completely serious I continued, "I'm just trying to, you know, I'm just trying to clean up man. That's all. It ain't nothing to do with you or anybody else. It's just time."

His smile faded and he nodded, probably realizing he had crossed the line. He paused for a moment and then said, "All right man. But we got to get together sometime and do something."

"We can do that . . . no problem."

He nodded again and then looking down the street he finally said, trying to leave on a laugh, "Well okay Mr. Party Pooper, don't be a stranger."

"Scouts honor," I joked back.

He grinned again, turned and walked back down the street.

When I reached the front door I pulled out my keys and paused as the ring on my finger caught my eye in the porch light. I turned and looked at Marcus walking away.

You're old lady ain't even around!

After I closed the door behind me and put the keys in their usual spot on the mantle, I started twisting my wedding, wandering what Sadie would say if she knew I told Marcus no.

8

An Opportunity to Teach

I woke up early on Sunday for no real reason other than I couldn't sleep anymore. When I opened the shades in the bedroom, the sun immediately brightened up the room and the first feeling I felt was panic. Not just nerves, but a real panic. It was the first day since getting out that the majority of the day wasn't planned out for me.

The rest of the previous week had been busy and manageable. My days usually stayed the same, except for the mornings I was able to go and see Danielle. Mr. Krueger allowed me to work extra hours on Friday and Saturday because the store was staying busy. As far as bosses went, he was pleasant enough to work for; he was respectful and not overly demanding. I was also getting a better feel for the store and knew my way around. As more and more customers would ask me for assistance, Mr. Krueger would let me help them. He was building trust in me.

After I finished breakfast, I sat in the living room watching the cars pass and wondered what I would do for the remainder of the day after leaving St. Joseph's. I really wanted to see Danielle, but I couldn't see her on the weekends because of Sadie.

The orphanage was becoming an important part of my day. I was getting to know my way around the kitchen and didn't have to worry about messing anything up; Sister Catherine made sure of that. It allowed me about two hours to kind of let go, enjoy the surroundings, and as crazy as it might sound, it gave me the opportunity to talk to Dee.

The first few days, I have to admit, her visits started to grate on me. I was brand new and did not want to have too much contact with anybody. If I was only going to be there a month, in my mind, it wasn't worth it. But there was no way to avoid her.

Every day, without fail, she would find her way over to my table in the back and start gabbing about someone or something. It was hard for me to be rude or turn her away. She allowed me to eat my lunch since she did most of the talking. When she would come over to the table and start I couldn't help but listen to her, drowning out the rest of the sounds around me. She was very smart and actually pretty funny at times.

Mostly she would discuss her ups and downs of orphanage life, which sister was this or that, and who she was friends with one day and enemies with the next. Most of the talking had revolved around her with little mention of me or my personal life, which was good. We both were getting comfortable with each other.

"Where were you yesterday?" she asked, kind of perturbed. She placed Reginald on the table and waited for a response. I had to laugh.

"I don't come on Saturdays because I have to go to work early." In the best sarcastic tone I could muster, I said, "I sure hope you made it through lunch okay."

She pursed her lips and replied, "Ha, ha."

"I've never asked and I guess I should, seeing as how it's gotten to be a habit. Are you sure it's okay for you to leave the other kids to come and sit with me everyday at lunch?"

"Sister Meredith doesn't care. I think she likes it when I leave to talk to someone else. I think she thinks I'm annoying," she answered, glancing in the direction of her lunch table.

I could have said something snide, but I just nodded.

"What kind of work do you do Lewis?" she asked.

"Well," I started, putting down my chicken salad sandwich. "I work over at a hardware store in town."

"Do you like it?"

"Sure, it's okay."

"How long have you worked there?"

"I started the same day I started here."

"Why would your boss let you come over here during the middle of the day?" she continued to probe.

"I just work at the hardware store during the afternoon."

She nodded and looked around the lunchroom. I took another bite of my sandwich.

"Are you married?"

"Uh, yes I am," I answered, a little unsure about the direction the questions were going.

"I bet she's really nice," Dee replied.

For a moment, I forgot the setting, and almost asked her about her family to try and get the subject off of me. Thankfully, I stopped myself before putting my foot in my mouth. She quickly changed the subject anyway.

"Do you know how to play chess?"

A little puzzled by the question I replied, "Where did that come from?"

"Just, do you know how to play—yes or no?"

"Yes I do, but it's been a while. Why?"

On her face came a pretty fierce scowl as she looked over at one of the boy's lunch tables. "Jessie Howard, that's why," she answered, still peering.

"So is he one of your *good* friends?" I asked. She turned her peer on me. I laughed. "I'm just kidding. What about Jessie Howard makes you so mad at him?"

"All he does is pick on girls all the time." Her face curled up and she talked in her best boy voice. *"I'm better at this; you can't do that; you don't even know what chess is."* The distortion on her face subsided. "He's just a bully that I would love to put in his place. He said that girls don't know how to play chess and I told him he was full of it."

I interjected and asked, *"Do* you know how to play chess?"

"No," she answered, deflated. "But he thinks I do, so now he says we have to play sometime to really see who can win. I need somebody to teach me," she said, looking up at me again.

"Well, I sure would like to help, but I don't think you'd be able to learn just by us talking at little bit after lunch. It would take a while."

"That's okay," she said, putting her legs up in her chair so she could sit on them. "I figure if you just show me how to play, we have an old chess table in the girl's room that nobody uses. I already checked and none of the other girls know how to play. It's just been sitting up there probably forever with nobody using it. Anyway, if you can just show me how to do it, I can practice with that table. It wouldn't take up that much time."

"Would you be able to bring the table down here?" I asked.

"Well, that's the problem. I don't think the sisters would let me just bring it down here from the second floor everyday for lunch. I was hoping if you knew how to play you might have a smaller one that you could show me on and then I would just practice with the big one."

Her eyes were pleading. How could I resist. "I can't promise you, but I'll see if I can find one. Is that okay?"

"Yes," she answered, as if saying a small prayer that I would be able to find one. The bell to end lunch rang and the kids started to scatter about.

"Remember, I'll see what I can do and I'll let you know tomorrow," I told her before she left.

56

"I sure hope so. I'll see you tomorrow," she replied, picked up Reginald, and started to leave. She suddenly stopped in her tracks, turned around, and held up her pinkie finger.

"You pinkie swear that you'll try to get one?"

"What?" I asked, confused.

"Hold out your pinkie," she commanded. I did and then she wrapped hers around mine in a sort of mini-handshake. "That's a pinkie swear."

I nodded and said, "I'll do the best I can." She hurried to catch up with the rest of her class.

As I walked toward the kitchen to put my tray away I wasn't sure how much I would be able to help her. I knew there wasn't a chess set at my house, but I knew where to get one. I just wasn't sure if my mother would let me borrow it.

9

Giving

When I left the orphanage I was so excited that Dee had asked me about chess. It had been a while since I had played and I wasn't sure if I remembered everything. By the time I started for my mother's house on Monday morning, the substitute chess board and pieces I had made out of the scrap paper in the house had been pretty well worn out. It wasn't much, but it kept me busy and gave me something to look forward to. That's all that I needed to get through the rest of Sunday.

Unlike normal, Danielle wasn't outside playing. I made it all the way to the front step before anybody acknowledged me. My mother came to the door.

"Danielle's out back with one of her friends," she said.

I nodded and stood on the top step. "How are you doing mama?"

"Fine." She paused for a second and wiped her hands on her apron. "How are things with you?" Again, there was no real emotion in her voice, but at least she asked.

"Things are going good. My job at the hardware store is doing good and being at the orphanage isn't as bad as I thought." I looked out across the yard. I wanted to say something about me not drinking, but decided not to bring it up.

"Well, if you want to see Danielle she's in the back, or I can just tell her you came by," she said, getting ready to turn and go back inside.

"Wait, mama, I actually . . . there was something I needed to ask you."

She stopped and waited.

"There is one of the kids at the orphanage who would like to learn how to play chess and I told her that I might be able to help her. Is there any way . . . I was hoping that I might be able to borrow dad's chess set?" I asked, hesitantly.

"I don't see why not, nobody's using it around here. As long as you don't let anything happen to it," she answered. "You're not going to leave it there are you?"

"I'll make sure not to. I'll just take it with me when I go and then bring it home. And it will just be until I can find another one that I might be able to use."

Without saying anything she turned around and walked back into the house. I waited on the porch.

She returned to the door holding the chess set. "I guess it's still got all the pieces to it." I walked up and opened the screen door and took it from her.

"I really appreciate this mama and promise that nothing will happen to it," I said, paused for a moment, and then without thought reached out to give her a hug. She didn't stop me, but she didn't really hug back either. I was willing to take it.

"I love you," I said as I backed up and let the screen door close.

She avoided the remark and asked, "Are you gonna say hi to Danielle?"

"I'll walk around back and at least say hello." She walked back into the house. I walked off the porch toward the back.

60

I really wanted to hold a grudge against her; I wanted to be mad at her. But, I just couldn't.

Just like me, she was taking steps.

❖   ❖   ❖

"Just how important is a pinkie swear?" I asked Dee as she sat down at the table.

"It's the most serious promise you can make. You didn't forget the chess set, did you?" she asked, concerned.

"Oh good," I said dramatically, "then I feel better for not forgetting."

She exhaled with relief. "That wasn't funny!"

"Do you even know how to set it up?" I asked, pulling out the wooden box that contained the chess pieces. The wooden box folded shut with metal clasps on the side to hold it together. When folded, there was empty space on the inside where all the pieces fit. When unfolded, the outside of the box lay flat on the table and became the chess board.

"I don't have a clue."

I started pulling the pieces out and placing them on the table. "Okay, here are all the pieces. Do you know any of the names?"

She looked over the pieces as she bit on her fingernail to concentrate. She pointed at the rook. "Is this the castle?" she asked hesitantly.

"Uh, kind of," I replied. "It's actually called a rook, but a castle will work. Any others?"

"Um," her finger slowly moved over the different pieces, "isn't there a king and a queen somewhere?"

I pulled them out for her. "The king and the queen," I said, placing them on the board.

"And here's a horse," she said, picking up the knight.

"Again, that's close enough. To play Jessie, we don't have to get extremely technical."

"Now just show me what I have to do to beat him," she said impatiently.

"I'm afraid it's not that easy Dee. There's a lot involved in

61

each game. First we have to set up the board."

"What?"

"First we have to set up the board," I repeated and started to move pieces around.

"I have to remember where each one of the pieces goes?" she exclaimed in dread, realizing that she wasn't going to gain a perfect understanding of the game on her first try.

"Do you want me to try and show you or not?"

"Yes," she said flustered, "I just don't know how I'm going to remember all of it."

"Well, like you said, you just need to know enough to show him that you know how to play. You don't necessarily have to beat him, right?"

"Yeah," she said disappointed.

"Well then all you need to know is the basics. You can at least show him that *girls* know how to play. Then you can practice and maybe beat him later."

"I guess you're right," she said with a little more confidence.

"So first, you need to know how to set up the board. Actually," I said, thinking over my teaching strategy. "Actually, the first thing you need to know, which is of vital importance, is that you are the king," I said and placed one of the kings in front of her.

A look of pain came across her face. "I don't want to be the king!"

"Well you have to be the king."

"Well I don't want to be the king! Can't I be the queen and Jessie be the king?"

I took in a deep breath and exhaled.

10

A Better Understanding

"How was St. Joseph's today?" Mr. Krueger asked as I walked through the door. Each day he opened up and became a little more social.

A couple of times, when the store had been slow, I wanted to ask him about his family, just to try and find out more about him. Maybe it was the fact he knew more about me than I did about him that got to me sometimes. But I never found the courage to ask about him or the picture on the back desk. Whenever I got the notion to ask, I would listen to my gut when it said, 'It's none of your business.'

"It was good Mr. Krueger," I answered, walking over to fill out my time card. "How has your day been?"

"Nothing special, but I would like to talk with you before you leave. Make sure you see me before you go, okay?" he asked.

"I'll be sure too."

The day flew by with customers coming in and out and

plenty of shelves to straighten out and stock. Over the week I had been there I began to feel more accountable, more responsible for the work I was doing.

When I had finished, I found him as quick as I could, curious as to what he wanted to say.

"I'm about to take off Mr. Krueger. You said you needed to see me." He was at the register, straightening out one of the displays.

"Yes Lewis. I just wanted to take a moment to let you know how much I appreciate your help in the store. You've been doing a great job."

"Thanks Mr. Krueger. I feel like I'm getting the hang of everything."

"Good, good," he said as he picked up my time card. "I was looking over your time card and it seems that if you work the same hours this week as last week that you should be done with what you owe me by Friday, maybe sooner. And as we mentioned when you started working, I can use some help around here. Business is good and steady, and having someone here on a regular basis would make it easier for me."

Since the first day of work the possibility of getting hired by Mr. Krueger full time had been in the back of my mind. What had started as a test, a trial on my part to see if anything was even possible, had steadily grown to a desire to be successful.

"I just wanted to let you know that if you can keep working hard and showing up on time, that this Saturday will be your first day of working for full pay if you want it," he said and then waited for a response.

I tried to hold it back, but I was smiling from ear to ear. "That would be great Mr. Krueger."

"That's good to hear. For now, you can keep the same hours because I know you have to continue helping out at the orphanage. But come next month I have some plans that might make things a little more hectic around here and I would need you around all day every day. Is that something you could do?"

"Most certainly Mr. Krueger."

64

"All I ask is that . . ." he took a second to gather his thoughts, "all I ask is that you *keep* doing what you've *been* doing," he said slowly, with a strong inflection, handing me my time card.

I got the message. I filled out my card for the day, put up my apron, and walked out of the store. I had made it one week on my own without anything to drink, and had a full time job to show for it.

I wanted to celebrate, but I didn't know how—at least not without drinking. In my heart, I wanted to go running to mom's house and find Sadie to tell her everything. To show her that I did it. But I wasn't ready for that either.

So I ended up doing thee same thing I did most nights, walking home by myself. Confirmation that I was heading in the right direction—that maybe I could do it—seemed like reward enough.

❖   ❖   ❖

"So what's the horsey thing do," Dee asked impatiently.

"Wait a minute Dee. Don't grab anything just yet; let me get the board set up." She fidgeted with her fingers as I set up the board. "Do you remember the names from yesterday?"

After doing a quick glance around the cafeteria, she pulled Reginald closer to her and moved his scarf to the side. As she did, she stuck her thumb and pointy finger into him like pinchers and pulled out a small piece of paper that had been folded up. I looked on curiously.

"It's my secret hiding place. It ain't much, but it's nice to have for emergencies," she said in a hushed voice of youthful seriousness.

"I bet it is," I said, trying not to laugh.

She unfolded the paper where she had been keeping notes from our lessons. After looking over it for a moment, she said, "Okay, this one is called the castle. This one is the king . . . the one that looks like it has a little hat on top. Oh, and all these guys up in the front are called ponds."

I tried not to laugh, but it slipped passed my lips.

"What's so funny?" she demanded defensively.

"Nothing . . . nothing. You almost had it right. They are called *pawns*, not *ponds*."

"Okay. So these are the *pawns*," she said with precision. "This is the rook, this is the horse, this is the bishop, and then the queen."

"That's good. Now," I continued, the pieces all set up, "what is the object of the game."

"All you have to do is," she said extending her hand to touch the king. She stopped herself and looked at me. I nodded for her to continue and she picked up the king. "You want to get the other person's king, right?"

"That's right. Each of the pieces moves different ways. The point is to try and take away the others person's pieces to give you a better chance of getting their king."

Her hands were cupped under her chin for the remaining eighteen minutes. Amazingly, not a word escaped her lips; she just listened and moved her pieces when I told her to. Since she had remembered the names, she needed to learn how they could move. She didn't get them all, but she got most of them. It was more than I had expected.

"It's almost time for lunch to be done. That was pretty good."

"I think I'm getting the hang of it. I've played other grown up games before, but never chess. Would you say this is kind of a grown up game?"

"Not necessarily. You just have to be patient. Don't worry, you'll get it," I said to encourage her.

She picked up one of the pawns to look at it, "Did you make these pieces? They look like somebody cut them out of wood."

"No, it was a chess set my father made a number of years ago."

"That's pretty nice of him to let you borrow it like this, especially if he made it. Do you see him often?"

I started putting the pieces away inside the box. "No, not really," I answered honestly. I almost finished the sentence, but I didn't

She folded up her piece of paper, put it back inside her secret spot behind Reginald's scarf and shook my hand. "Either way, it was still nice of him to let you borrow it." I watched as she walked away with her class.

She left me sitting there with a lump in my throat and the only thing I had in my possession to remember my father. Since the talk with Judge Sanders, the day after I got out of jail, it was the first time I had mentioned him. Even when I was alone—especially when I was alone—I tried not to think about him. His death was so sudden, unexpected. A heart attack at forty six.

I could feel my chest start to warm on the inside so I quickly picked up my tray and the chess set to leave. The orphanage cafeteria was not where I wanted to have a breakdown.

"Mr. Anderson, Mr. Anderson." Sister Maria came waddling into the cafeteria. "Mr. Anderson, Ms. Weston would like a word with you if you have a moment."

I nodded, told Sister Catherine I needed to leave, and listened to her complain as I followed Sister Maria down the hallway to the administrative offices. As I walked through the door Ms. Weston lowered a piece of paper she was studying.

"Lewis thanks for taking the time. Please have a seat." I sat down, putting the chess set in the chair next to me. I could tell she was searching for a way to say whatever was on her mind.

"Lewis, I need to talk to you about something. I need to talk to you about Dee," she stated and then waited for a reaction.

Not sure what reaction she was after, I asked, "What about her?"

"Well Lewis, it has come to my attention that you two have become quite the pair and that she spends the end of her lunch time with you at your table. Is that correct?" Her hands were clasped and her tone was friendly, yet concerned.

I didn't think I had done anything wrong, though my conscience started nagging at me for not asking someone sooner if it was okay. "Yes ma'am. She just kind of came over and introduced herself and keeps coming over each day. I don't mind if she comes over, but I guess I should have asked if it was okay. Is there something wrong with her stopping by my table?"

"No, there's nothing wrong, per se, I just wanted to follow up on it." She rose, walked in front of her desk, and sat in one of the seats against the wall, diagonal to me.

"Mr. Anderson, when Judge Sanders told me you were coming to do service I have to admit I was somewhat leery."

Surprised, I started. "I thought that . . ."

"You thought I didn't know about Judge Sanders or why you were here, didn't you?" she said softly.

Feeling somewhat foolish, I nodded.

"It's okay Mr. Anderson, you do not have to worry or be surprised. If you weren't going to bring it up I wasn't going to make you. But, I will let you know that I work very hard to know who comes and goes out of St. Joseph's."

"Ms. Weston, I was never trying to hide anything from you. I guess I figured it didn't matter why I was here, as long as I was doing my work and not causing any trouble," I said in a small tone of defensiveness.

"In most cases anyone wanting to give service is more than welcome, but I have a special responsibility since there are children involved. This is why I was a little cautious at first.

"Since you've been here, everything Judge Sanders said about you has been completely accurate and I have had nothing to worry about. Your recent past has been, for lack of a better term, lacking stability. Is that a fair assessment?"

"Yes ma'am, at least before going to see Judge Sanders. But, since then, things have been more stable and I've been following what Judge Sanders has asked me to do. It's been . . ." I hesitated to tell her. Saint Joseph's played a role in what seemed like my life heading in a positive direction and I didn't want to mess it up. I concluded that I needed to be honest. "It's been over a month since I've really had anything to drink." I felt a small amount of achievement.

"I'm glad to hear it." She rose again and walked back behind her desk. "These kids need every moment of a positive male role model in their life that they can get, especially Dee."

"I can understand your concern Ms. Weston, about being unstable and all, but I assure you I have nothing but good intentions. I can't say I was excited to do it at first, but over this last week the kids have really rubbed off on me, especially Dee. It's really good for me coming here and I look forward to it . . . Sister Catherine aside."

She laughed a little and nodded, then continued. "Dee extended the hand of friendship to you so openly and honestly; she's unlike any child I have ever met. Maybe that's what I find so interesting about her. She is special."

I decided to interject and push the issue. "I'm not sure if you're allowed to talk about it, but what happened to her parents?"

She did not hesitate. "As you may have noticed most of the children in here, have lost, at least momentarily, any hope in their lives. Where love had come, or at least should have come, unconditionally, it now comes from strangers."

Her chair squeaked in the silence as she sat down. The wrinkles in her face were a little more noticeable. She seemed unusually tired and was not afraid to let her guard down. "What little joy they find comes from the sisters. Eventually, if they're not adopted—which unfortunately only about half of them ever are—they enter the working world at sixteen or seventeen with nobody. It almost seems fruitless sometimes.

"Then there's Dee. I think you summed it up well—I've never met any other girl like her. In fact, I can say I've never really met *anybody* like her. She is able to pull her hope from the inside, somewhere down deep. It's like she knows something; something that nobody else does, and it keeps her going."

"How long has she been here?" I asked.

"I guess it's been almost six months or so. She showed up on the doorstep around the beginning of the year and didn't have anywhere else to go. She had some clothes, that bear she carries around with her, and that was it. It's not uncommon for kids to wind up here after being on their own; word gets around when kids are on the street that there is somewhere they can go. Even as young as twelve or thirteen or however old she is.

"You see, we don't even know her exact age. We don't even know if Dee is her real name. It's all just kind of guess work. We've tried to put pieces together, but from what we can gather she has suffered through some very traumatic experiences and only remembers bits and pieces."

She leaned forward in her chair and continued, "According to her, she was at home, in the winter, with her mother, grandmother and brother. Her father came home late one night and we assume turned on the kerosene heater without lighting the pilot. She woke up the next morning and found them all, suffocated by carbon monoxide."

She was shaking her head at me as she spoke, knowing my thoughts. "I know it's hard to believe, but it's been the same story over and over again. Her room was the only one with a window open. It gave her a supply of fresh air. She says all she can remember is that she left it open for her dad. For some reason she says he wasn't supposed to come around the house, but she would leave the window open for him to come in on nights it got real cold. From her remembering he didn't actually live there. He apparently thought it was too cold, but didn't know how, or wasn't in any condition, to work the heater. She remembers waking up, finding her family like that, grabbing her bear, and running."

I was captivated. I couldn't take my eyes off Ms. Weston as she spoke. "But how did she . . ."

She interrupted, "After that Dee said she doesn't remember anything until she was at a halfway house in the city and heard about us last Christmas and made her way here. She says she doesn't know her last name or anymore than that; whether or not she's lying we don't know. Even if she is lying, it doesn't matter. If we don't know the truth for sure, we just kind of have to take her word for it and help her out the best we can. When kids get cold and desperate, they'll do anything for clothes and shelter.

70

"We had authorities search high and low for such an incident as one she mentioned, or anything even remotely similar, across ours and neighboring states and we found nothing. We put pictures out at all the halfway houses in the city too and that was not help."

"But that doesn't make any sense?" I said, finding it hard to believe. "A young girl like that basically making it on her own and then just winding up here somehow."

"I grant it's unique, but it's not the first time. We have a few children here that, as I mention, just show up on our door. We do the best we can with what we have. We don't know who her relatives are or what the whole, factual history is. Supposedly she doesn't know either. Maybe its better off that way and we can give her a brand new start," she said in a quiet moment of questioning and honesty.

I nodded, still in complete astonishment at the story I had heard.

"Can you imagine?"

Realizing that she had probably said more than she should, Ms. Weston composed herself and took a deep breath.

"Anyway, Mr. Anderson, that's a little background. It's strictly confidential of course. I assume I have your confidence?"

"Yes ma'am."

"Thank you. And as I mentioned, any positive male role models she can be around is good for her. To put it in simple terms though, I just need your word that you will keep this relationship in a proper perspective and only visit with Dee in the lunchroom as you have been," she concluded, and looked directly at me, waiting for my answer.

"That's not a problem Ms. Weston. And I appreciate you telling me, I didn't know."

"Very good then. Thank you for your time with me today and thank you for your service to the children."

"Thanks Ms. Weston." I quietly removed myself from her office and into the hallway.

I left through the large double doors in the front foyer. The view was as beautiful as the first day I came.

My respect for Ms. Weston had grown. With her ability to look past the outer shell, she truly wanted to make a difference. Hearing her tell Dee's story—personalizing it a little—allowed some of her emotion, some of her desire to help, to rub off on me. Even if I wasn't more than a server for the other kids, maybe I could make a positive difference for Dee.

11

A Matter of Time

Days were starting to run together, which was good. It felt good to realize I was giving again. It's important to feel needed I guess—even if it is just teaching chess and helping at a hardware store.

I left the house and passed the tree lined streets, Ms. Weston's words weighing on my mind.

I really wanted to see Danielle.

I really wanted to see Sadie, too.

Sadie.

So far it was the only aspect of my life that didn't seem to be heading in a positive direction. But I couldn't think about it. It was on her terms. Trying to do something or pushing the issue would make worse.

Besides, if I was going to try anything I would need more time; more proof that I could do it on my own. She would need that reassurance.

When I reached the drive at my mother's house and looked up at the porch that little voice inside of me told me to

turn around and leave.   As soon as I saw Ruth Hannigan, it
spoke to me loud and clear.

Mrs. Hannigan didn't think much of me and, well, I didn't
think much of her. She was basically the town gossip. The
only reason I think she visited my mother was the good
source material it provided.

"Well goodness, Rebecca, I still can't believe every time I
see him how he used to just be a little ol' thing and now look
how big he is," she said in a stinging, high pitched voice.

I cringed inside. "Hello mama. Good morning Mrs.
Hannigan. It's been a while."

"It sure has, Lewis," she replied, pausing between each
word, drawing the phrase out.

My mother just sat there and waited for one of us to say
something else.

"I don't want to interrupt, just wanted to visit with
Danielle for a few minutes before heading off to the
orphanage," I said, trying to remove myself from harms way.

Mrs. Hannigan's eyes got wide. "The orphanage . . . you
mean St. Joseph's? What are you doing over there?"

"I'm helping serve lunch to the children."

"It's part of his probation from his last lock up with Judge
Sanders, you know, to help give back to the community," said
my mother very matter-of-factly to Mrs. Hannigan, as if it
was just something to add to the conversation.

Mrs. Hannigan gave an 'oh' with the nod of her head and
then a smile for me as to approve of my public service. I was
boiling on the inside.

"I really don't think that's anybody's concern mama," I
semi-barked, trying to contain my composure. The pressure
was building up and I could feel it wanting to come out.

Mom's eyes got cold and Mrs. Hannigan's eyes got even
bigger. They were both staring at me and there was an
awkward silence. I wasn't sure what direction my mother
would go. Mrs. Hannigan just continued to fan herself, mouth
agape, and turned to look at my mother.

She kept her eyes on me when she finally spoke. "You
listen to me! It's the one positive thing I've been able to say
about you in a long time. I know it ain't much to say, but at
least you've been sticking with it for almost two weeks now.

I'm sorry if it doesn't sound positive to you—that's not my problem. So you better just get off our high horse worrying about what other people think about you. If you're worried so much then do something about it!"

Her head snapped away from me and turned back to look out over the yard. Mrs. Hannigan loved every minute of it and turned to look out over the yard as well, showing support for my mother.

Do something about it!

The words enraged me.

"I am doing something about it!" I shouted back.

Their heads turned back to me, surprised. I was still on the steps, but leaned forward some to grab the railing. "I'm doing everything I know to do about it. I've been out for almost two weeks and I've been keeping busy. I've been working hard at Krueger's. I'm going to even start getting a full wage." I lowered my voice as their eyes remained fixed. "I haven't had anything to drink. Not one drop since I've been out. I don't know what else you want me to do!"

Mrs. Hannigan looked at my mother to see what she would do next. I could tell by the look on Mrs. Hannigan's face that even though she wanted to side with my mother, she supported my logic.

My mother waited, and then replied, "Danielle's not here; she stayed at a friend's house last night. Sorry you came all this way for nothing."

I ran my fingers through my hair and exhaled. It was okay for her to embarrass me in front of her friend, but there was no way she was going to admit that I did the same to her.

"Yeah, me too."

I made my way back down the drive and left them there where I had found them.

❖   ❖   ❖

"Hurry up Lewis!" Sister Catherine bellowed as I was getting the rolls out of the oven.

"I'm hurrying!" I yelled back. The kitchen staff froze and Sister Catherine shot me a glaring look. I gave her one right

75

back and continued pulling the rolls out. It was the worst I had felt since Sadie came to see me in jail.

When the children were finally served I sat with my food and tried to calm down a bit. But the more I tried to forget what my mother said, the more I didn't want to let it go.

"Are you going to eat it or stare at it?"

Dee had snuck up beside me. I lowered my fork and half faked a smile. She placed a plastic chess set on the table.

"Look what I finally got!" she said, holding up a chess set. "I borrowed it from Adam Harper. He said he never uses it anyway. Plus, I think he wants me to beat Jamie," she said with a wry smile.

I still didn't respond. Dee started to take the pieces out of the box.

"It's not quite as fancy as your dad's, but that way you won't have to lug it around and . . ."

"Today might be a good day for a break Dee," I interjected.

She stopped and looked up. "What do you mean?"

"I mean, I'm not really feeling up to it today, if that's okay?"

The joy in her face left, though she tried to hide it. "Uh, yeah, I guess that's okay." She started putting the chess pieces slowly back in the box.

"I promise it's just for today Dee. Just a rough morning that's all."

"It's no problem," she said, putting the top on the box and looking up at me. "Is there anything I can do to help?"

"No, I don't think so," I replied, trying to bring my fork up to my mouth again to take another bite. I dropped it back on the plate.

"I don't think I've ever seen you in a bad mood before."

I returned her honesty. "Well, I think this is the first one I've had in quite a while."

"Do you want to know what I do when I get in a bad mood?" she asked.

"Not really," I said bluntly. As the words rolled off my tongue, I realized how it sounded. Her eyes filled with hurt.

"That's fine. I really do hope you feel better, Lewis." She got up and walked away with the chess set. A part of me wanted to stop her, but a bigger part of me just let her go. I just wanted to be alone and realizing that I upset her just gave me all the more reason to sit with my guilt.

❖   ❖   ❖

I didn't say more than three things at Mr. Krueger's— 'hello', 'goodbye', and 'thank you'.

At the end of my shift I put my apron back where it belonged, washed my hands and made my way out the front when Mr. Krueger called me over to the register.

"Lewis, I've got something for you before you leave." I walked over to him, not responding. He handed me a five dollar bill.

"I know it's not much," he continued, "but you are officially all paid up and that's the left over from the rest of this week so far." He pointed to the time card lying on the table.

Rolling the money between my fingers, my mood started to change a little.

Do something about it!

I was and the proof was right here. I smiled for the first time all day.

"Thank you Mr. Krueger," I said softly and put the five in my pocket.

The register chimed as he closed it. "Keep up the good work Lewis. You've been a great help and I look forward to great things to come," he finished, extending his hand. I shook it firmly and then headed out the door. It was cloudier than normal, but still warm.

"Lewis! Hey, Lewis!" I heard someone yelling from across the street. I looked over and saw Marcus making his way through the traffic. It had been over a week since we last saw each other. I braced, not knowing what to expect.

"Hey man, what's up? What are you doing down this way?" he asked with the same care free charm I had always known. Apparently, our last encounter didn't hold any long term impact on him.

"I'm just heading home from work."

"Oh yeah, that's right, the hardware store," he said nodding. "How's that going?" he asked.

"It's still going good," I answered with a smile as I started to warm up to the notion of seeing him again. He nodded back. "What are you up to?"

"I was heading down to Charlie Kingston's. They're having a party for him. Something about getting promoted at work or something; at least that's what I heard." I tried to hold in my grin. It was just like Marcus; all he had to hear was the word 'party' and he was there.

"Hey man, you should come with me!" he exclaimed, as if he had received a revelation. "You probably know Charlie better than I do and that way I don't have to look like a moocher just coming by myself. What do you say?" he asked, his eyes big with encouragement.

I stalled and lowered my head, "I'm not sure man."

"Look Lewis," he said a little more serious, "I get where you're coming from with the trying to stop drinking; that's all cool. But I mean, it ain't like we can't still hang out and stuff. And something like this," he took a second to gather his thoughts, "at somebody's house it will be a bit more respectable and all. I mean, the sun's still out. Not like we're going out at all hours of the night."

I looked up at him. He had a point. If there was any time to hang out, something like this would be better.

"Look man," he said, putting his hand on my shoulder, "just come. I promise I won't ask you to drink nothing. I mean you gotta do something, right? You can't just keep going home every night and sitting there. Come on—we won't even stay long." he said, turning me gently with his hand as he started walking in his initial direction.

My feet hadn't moved yet. He walked ahead of me a few paces.

I couldn't help but follow Marcus's logic. I didn't have to drink. He said he wouldn't encourage me and I believed him. It would be a different setting than going out to a bar or club. Charlie wasn't somebody either one of us knew too well, but we had all gone to school together. It wouldn't be completely out of the ordinary if we showed up.

Do something about it!

The thought rang through my head one last time and I felt

I *had* to go. If I went to a social event where I knew there would be drinking and I didn't drink then I *would* have done something about it. Then maybe she would be happy. Then maybe I would have passed the test with Sadie.

I was ready to find out.

"Why not?" I said with a smile and smacked Marcus on the back. He whooped and hollered for what must have been a whole city block as we headed toward Charlie Kingston's so-called promotion party.

12

Beginning Again

The bright sun tore through my eyes as I stepped off the bus. I tried to read the road sign but it took a minute to regain focus. Usually, I would have taken a right to head down to Mr. Krueger's, but seeing as I was going to be late anyway, there was something I needed to do first.

I turned left and made my way up the couple of blocks to Stanton Road, turned left again and went four blocks. Then a right on Millway and a left on Otterdale to 9436 – Judge Sanders house.

I was still fully dressed when I woke that morning. The alarm clock didn't go off because I didn't remember to set it. I didn't remember getting into bed. I didn't remember opening the door. I didn't remember getting home.

I closed my eyes. My head was pounding. I didn't want to remember anything about the situation, or any situation like it. I wanted to be done. I thought I was.

When I went with Marcus the night before, I felt like I

was ready to turn that corner. My mind telling my body that I could handle it; that I was strong. That I had something to prove.

I was wrong.

And that morning, when I finally got over feeling sorry for myself, the only thing I could think to do—that I *needed* to do—was to talk to Judge Sanders. As much as I owed to Mr. Krueger and as much as I didn't want to be late, he could wait.

It had taken a little tracking down, but when I finally found his address I couldn't get there fast enough. Like a saint ready to confess his sins, I was ready to spill everything at his feet and await his penance.

After a few seconds a woman appeared at the screen. She was middle-aged, healthy, with dark hair wearing a gardening apron. Her hands and the apron were stained with dirt.

"Yes sir, may I help you," she said with a polite, yet cautious tone, as if she did not expect company. I'm sure my ragged appearance didn't help any.

"Mrs. Sanders?" I asked.

"Yes," she said hesitantly.

"Yes ma'am, I was hoping Judge Sanders might be home?"

"He is, but he's rather busy at the moment and isn't used to taking calls at home. Is he expecting you?"

"Um, no ma'am, he's not. I hate to just show up like this, but if you could please tell him that it's Lewis Anderson and if he wouldn't mind, I sure could use a few minutes of his time," I said with a hint of desperation.

She nodded respectfully and disappeared back into the house. I turned on the small concrete porch to view the rest of the street. The neighborhood was quiet. The Sander's brick rancher was modest in size but extremely well kept. The grass on the front lawn was lush. There were perfectly shaped hedges, patches of colorful flowers and everything seemed right in its place.

I heard footsteps coming back toward the door. Mrs. Sanders seemed to approach with a little less apprehension.

"Yes Mr. Anderson, Mr. Sanders is around back and said that he can speak with you," she said with a smile. "You can just follow the path there to the right of the house," she said pointing.

"Thank you so much Mrs. Sanders," I said and started down the walk.

As I opened the gate, I stepped into an absolutely gorgeous backyard. To the left was a concrete patio directly out of the double sliding glass doors from the back of the house. The yard was flat and long, running back roughly 50 or 60 feet. It was fenced on all sides with a shed in the back right corner. Along the right side of the fence were more colorful flowers and blossoms. On the left side, towards the house, were some fruit trees, then a swing set and a picnic table, and in the back left corner, kneeling over what appeared to be a modest vegetable garden, was Judge Sanders.

As the gate rattled shut he got off his knees, wiped his forehead and hands on the small towel around his belt, and walked towards me. Nobody said anything until we met in the middle of the yard.

"Well good morning Lewis. This is a surprise," he said, extending his hand. I extended mine as the guilt suddenly rushed back into me.

"Lynette said you wanted to talk," he said solemnly. On the bus ride over, I had been replaying the last words I had spoken to him in his office the day I got out—I was sure he had not forgotten.

If I don't think I'll be able to do it, I'll gladly walk over to the jail myself and close the door behind me. You have my word.

At the time, I never thought I was going to make it two weeks.

"I'm really sorry for coming to see you at your home, Judge Sanders."

"That's okay Lewis, as long as you don't make it a habit," he said politely, but with a tone of seriousness.

I nodded, and continued, "Do you remember what I said in

83

your office the day I got out?"

He kept his eyes on me. "I do," he answered bluntly, not giving me anything else to feed off of. He was keeping the conversation on my terms, just like how I had left it.

"Well," I started, doing another glance around at the scenery, gathering my thoughts, "things have been going good . . . real good. The orphanage, Mr. Krueger's, and I've been basically sober for going on six weeks with absolutely nothing to drink for two . . .," I paused.

"Until?" he asked, finishing my sentence.

"Until last night," I said, the words coming hard. He nodded without much expression as the double glass doors opened up. Mrs. Sanders walked out with a tray of glasses and a pitcher of water. She carried them to the picnic table over by the swing set.

"Let's sit down," he said, placing his hand on my shoulder and steering me toward the table. His wife did not say anything as she placed the tray on the table and headed back in the house.

I followed him over to the table, trying to appear strong, but wrestling with myself on the inside. A part of me knew that I was at a different place, that I had come a long way. Unlike the last time I was with Judge Sanders, this time I sincerely *wanted* to make a change.

"Would you like some water?" he asked, pouring himself a glass.

"Sure," I said, not really thirsty.

"What happened?" he asked.

I started off with everything the previous morning, from the incidents at mom's that started it all, to the money from Mr. Krueger and running into Marcus. He kept his gaze on me and just let me talk.

I then continued on with what I remembered; there was nothing to hide. I remembered going with Marcus to Charlie's house. It was a pretty good crowd of people. It was more like a backyard type barbeque get together that everyone was invited to.

We got there and said congratulations to Charlie who was

happy to see us and made no fuss so we stuck around. Most of the food was already gone by the time we had gotten there, but there were lots of people we knew. I thought at first it would be nice to socialize and see some people I hadn't seen for a while. I had been lying low, trying to avoid all the questions I knew would come. But I was feeling confirmed, sure of my ability to handle it. I wanted to see if I could do it.

"It wasn't easy, was it?" he asked, interrupting.

I exhaled. "Not really. More than anything I just got sick of being the center of attention. I'll give it to Marcus, he kept his promise. He didn't try to get me to drink, but after a while it seemed like he wanted to show me off more than anything. I must have been the only adult there with a Coke in my hand . . . at least not with anything extra in it"

"Nothing's as awe worthy to a steady drinker I guess than somebody who's on the wagon," he said and we both took another drink. "Well, then what happened?"

"Actually, everything at the party was fine. We stayed for probably an hour or so; just long enough to talk and for Marcus to get a few drinks in him. The problem was trying to get home," I said, putting my glass back on the picnic table.

"Marcus wouldn't let you go would he?" Judge Sanders guessed.

I laughed involuntarily, even though it wasn't funny. And then shook my head. "No, actually, it really wasn't Marcus's fault. We were walking and just enjoying each others company. I have to admit it was nice to be around him sober. He's really not a bad guy, just has some things to work out, like we all do," I added, making sure I looked directly at Judge Sanders when I said it.

I continued to tell him what I remembered. I didn't feel like going home yet and I didn't mind hanging out with Marcus—I just didn't want to go to one of our old places. Then I remembered I had the five dollars from Mr. Krueger's and asked if he wanted to get something to eat since we missed out on the food at Charlie's.

We found a restaurant and sat down and had a real nice dinner—something we had never really done before. He did drink some more and got pretty tipsy, but he still kept his promise and didn't push me and I stayed strong.

After dinner we were just sitting around, having desert. He was pretty well gone and in a good mood it seemed. I was feeling on top of the world, and then he asked a question that changed everything, 'How's Sadie and your girl?'

I tried to keep eye contact with Judge Sanders as I continued the story, but it was hard. "Looking back, he was just making small talk, but I couldn't help it. Really feeling like I had proved something I just started gushing out everything. Things *had* been going better and I *had* been doing my part. I could get Sadie back; I knew it in my heart. I didn't care what my mom thought. I was staying sober and I knew I could keep doing it." Even retelling it, I started to get excited at the prospect.

Judge Sanders held up his hand to slow me down. "What did Marcus think about all the good things going on in your life?" he asked.

I clasped my hands together and put them back on the table. "He didn't seem as excited as I was. I think it . . . I think it kind of made him sad actually. Well, sad and mad. He just let me keep talking and I was all up on myself about all the things that were going to happen and that I was going to do."

"All the things he wasn't doing," Judge Sanders said quietly.

I nodded and took another drink. "It wasn't until I was done that I could tell something was wrong," I continued. "He said, real sarcastic, 'Wow, all that sounds great' and things like that. I tried to play it off and bring him back down, but I guess he was a little too gone. He eventually got mad and started yelling at me right there in the restaurant. 'You just think you're better than me.' He kept saying things like that before he finally stood up and said, 'can't you see that no matter what you do Sadie ain't coming back' and then he stormed out. Everyone watched him as he left and then I felt the eyes on me."

A fly landed on my hand. I shooed it away and then stood

86

up to pace.

"It was the first time somebody else had said it to me," I continued. I had thought it enough, and felt it. And even though he had been drinking when he said it, he meant it and I guess that was enough to get me thinking.

"I don't know why I just didn't get up and leave. I knew everyone was staring at me because of the argument; I could *feel* it. When I was drunk and people were looking I didn't care, mostly because I didn't have enough sense."

I looked directly at Judge Sanders. "For some reason Marcus just made me feel guilty enough . . . made me feel low enough and got me saying to myself that maybe Sadie wasn't coming back. I reached across the table and grabbed what was left of his beer."

When I said it a knot hit in my stomach and my throat clamped up. My hand involuntarily made a fist and I wanted to punch something.

"Was that all?" he asked.

I sat back down to try and relax again. "No. It didn't even taste good going down. It was warm. But it was like someone put off a firework inside me and everything lit up. I started sweating and it was like my insides were having a party and they were waiting for the main attraction to come. After that, I wasn't even thinking. I went down to the liquor store and got a whole bottle and took it home. I finished it there. Then I woke up this morning fully dressed, late for work and not sure what to do." I looked at him again.

"So now what do you do?" he asked, rather bluntly, without much emotion.

"Well," I hesitated, "that's why I came to talk to you. I . . . I wasn't sure what I should do."

"Do you think Marcus was right?" he asked, taking me by surprise.

"No," I finally said, not a hundred percent sure, but feeling good about the answer.

"So you think Sadie will take you back?"

"Eventually," I answered, "if . . . if I *really* quit drinking."

"If you really quit drinking," Judge Sanders repeated.

"What does that mean, *really*? Is there ever a real way to know if you've completely quit drinking; for good, forever?"

He looked at me and waited. "I guess not," I finally answered, a little disheartened as I realized that what he was saying made sense. "She'd just have to trust me."

He finally smiled. "That's what it is all about. You can make a promise, but the only one responsible for the outcome is you—it lies squarely on your shoulders. They have to utterly and completely trust you. And you," he said, pointing right at me, "have to utterly and completely realize that you have to play by a whole new set of rules in order to keep that trust."

There was a pause as he looked over toward the house at the sliding door where his wife had come out of earlier, "Because if keeping the trust in that relationship is important enough then you *will* play by the rules. But as soon as you don't care about the relationship, or have a reason not to worry about the trust, then you've lost."

He picked up his water glass and made a motion, as if making a toast, "Trust me." As he took his sip, I sat there and took it all in.

"So do *you* think I've still got a chance?" I asked.

"Lewis," he said, standing to stretch. "It doesn't matter what I think. But I will say this; I don't think you would have come over to talk to me if you didn't think you had a chance. If you thought it was over . . . if you thought last night would have been the last straw, then you would have either stayed in bed a depressed mess or you would have gone out and found some more booze."

He was right.

"It doesn't matter what I personally think, but as your judge I do have two suggestions," he said, motioning for me to walk with him back to the gate.

When we reached the gate he opened it and stood there, holding it with one hand, the other in his pocket. "Marcus might be a nice guy, but you don't need nice guys around you right now. It sounds like you were doing just fine before hanging out with him. And the second suggestion is to not be late at Mr. Krueger's again—I've heard you've been doing some good work and he's got big plans for you."

He stuck out his hand and shook it firmly, with confidence. "Thank you Judge Sanders. I really appreciate you taking the time to listen to me. And tell Mrs. Sanders thank you, too," I said humbly.

"It's no problem Lewis," he said as I turned and walked down the drive, a little more hopeful than when I arrived.

13

Letting Go

After I left Judge Sanders I went as quickly as I could over to Mr. Krueger's. I was an hour and a half late. My plan was to tell him everything as soon as I walked in the door, to hold nothing back, but he didn't give me the chance. As soon as the bell rang he looked up from the register where he was helping a customer and gave me directions straight away. He wasn't noticeably upset.

It was torture having to wait. I just wanted to get it off my chest, regardless of the consequences. I swept up, restocked, helped a few customers and tidied up the back for a couple of hours before the store slowed down. But I couldn't take it any longer. The first chance I got I took it. I wanted to be the first one to say something. He was in the front, helping a customer out the door.

"Uh, Mr. Krueger. I wanted to talk to you about this morning," I said, trying to be as sincere as possible. One thing the delayed confession did was give me time to gather my thoughts. "First off I want to apologize for being so late. It is not my intention to make that a habit."

He nodded in agreement.

I continued. "You have been nothing but fair and honest with me and have really helped me to get back on my feet. I know today was the first real day for me to be working full time. I was . . ." I paused. I had planned to tell him everything; it seemed like the right thing to do when I was thinking it through. But now that I was reciting, standing in front of him, something inside told me I had said enough. He didn't need anymore. I improvised, "it was wrong of me and I'll be more responsible."

He did not hesitate in his response. "I appreciate that Lewis. So far, you have been working great and doing a good job. Setbacks happen and things come up, sometimes we're late; I've been there. All I ask, like you said, is that it does not become a habit. Fair enough?"

"Fair enough"

"Tell you what," he continued, "check for restocking again, clean out the backroom for me and then you can have the rest of the day off. To be honest, and I don't mean this against you, but you don't look so good."

"I'm really feeling okay Mr. Krueger and am willing to stay. I don't mind," I insisted. Did he know the reason I was late? Was it obvious?

"No," he said flatly, "do what I asked and then go home and get some rest. I need you here in top form on Monday because we've got a lot to talk about."

A lot to talk about? That was news to me. It took me back. "A lot to . . ."

"Look, just get your work done and then go home and then I'll see you on Monday." It was very uncharacteristic of him to be so insistent.

"Okay Mr. Krueger," I said, defeated, making my way back into the storeroom. I walked over to the back door and opened it to let in some air. I ran my fingers through my hair and glanced around to see what needed to be done before leaving. The longer I stood there, taking a moment to rest, I realized maybe he was right—I didn't feel good. Sweat had gathered all on my face and back and my breathing was accelerating. I needed to get my work done, get home and lay down. The night before was catching up with me.

I felt like I couldn't stand any longer and reached over, grabbing the chair at the small work desk. Sitting down I caught a glimpse of the old photo and decided to take a closer look. As I took hold of it, the rounded, silver edge of the frame was cool to the touch.

They looked happy. As my fingers rolled up and down the side, I thought about Sadie and when we had been happy. I thought about Danielle. How much that loss must have meant to Mr. Krueger? How much she must have been a part of him; a part of the store?

Then I thought about dad.

I gripped the frame tight, just for a brief second, before I quickly put it back. My head and body were aching as I got back to finishing up my work.

❖   ❖   ❖

When I woke the next day—Sunday—it was early. After a cold bath, which felt painfully welcome against my sore muscles, I made some toast and eggs. But they just sat on the dining table, untouched. I went back and forth between looking at them and the picture of my father that was staring at me from the living room.

It was a small picture that sat on the corner table right next to the sofa. I'd seen it every day since moving back into the house, but never wanted to acknowledge it. I had ignored it, just like the picture of my mother on their wedding day that sat on the mantle next to where I placed my keys. I just brushed by them, not ready to deal with them—until now.

I slowly got up from the table, walked toward it, and really *looked* at it for the first time. The more his features came into gaze, the more it sank in how much I really missed him. I sat down on the couch next to the picture.

It was a body shot of my father from the waist up. He was dressed up nice for some occasion, long sleeve button up shirt and nice trousers. He wasn't frowning, but he wasn't necessarily smiling. I knew he had been happy though. He had always made the most of everything: honest, hard working, willing to help, humble. I had never heard anybody say one negative thing about my father my entire life.

I put the picture back down and looked around the room as the shadows of the morning were dancing around. He wasn't easy on me, but he was fair. He didn't indulge in much, but he loved fixing things, spending time with family . . . and chess. I smiled.

I only ever saw him cry two times in my life: when I got married and when Danielle was born. The feeling started in my chest and worked its way straight up my frame. He was always there for me. He never gave up on me.

The tears slowly, quietly fell into my lap as I sat on the couch and for the first time allowed myself to miss my dad.

❖   ❖   ❖

"So what's new?" Dee asked as she plopped herself down in front of me.

I was so glad to see her. We hadn't spoken since I brushed her off on Friday.

"Not much," wiping the extra apple sauce off the corner of my mouth. She had the chess board with her today, but didn't start taking the pieces out like she normally did. I had left my father's set at home.

"Dee, I really want to apologize for acting like I did on Friday. I know it wasn't very nice to just, well, kind of ignore you like that. I was having a rough day," I said sincerely.

She didn't flinch in her acceptance, waving it off with her hand, almost theatrically, "Don't even worry about it! We all have bad days, I guess. Besides, it's been real nice of you to take the time with me; so, I figured you had a day off coming anyway."

I smiled, grateful. "Thanks Dee. Do you have time today?" I asked.

Her eyes got big, "You bet I do!" She didn't skip a beat as she started pulling out the pieces and setting up the board. She kept talking. "I've been teaching one of the other girls, Melinda Fisher, to play too so I can have someone to practice with. I think I'm going to be ready to play Jamie real soon."

The board was complete and we started taking our turns. After a few minutes of playing she piped up, "Are you feeling better?" She didn't look at me, but kept looking at the board, as if she wasn't sure if she wanted to ask the question or not.

"Yeah, I am," I answered, feeling comfortable telling her. Our relationship had grown to the point where I didn't mind talking to her about me. She still didn't know about why I was there though—that was one thing I kept from her. "I . . . I just had a bad day on Friday. Started off bad with a little argument with my mom, that's all."

She nodded, showing she was listening, and then moved one of her pawns. I studied the board for a second and then placed my fingers on my bishop.

"Have you guys made up yet?" she asked. My fingers remained on the piece.

"Uh, not yet, but I'm going to go and see her tomorrow," I said, the words sounding right as they came out. It wasn't something I was looking forward to—not knowing how my mother would react—but it was something I needed to do. I finally moved my bishop.

Out of nowhere, Dee started laughing, filled with excitement. "What's the matter?" I asked, unsure.

"Can you do something for me?" she asked, still aglow with joy, her hand twitching to move at the board. I nodded. "Can you tell your dad I said thanks for letting you borrow his chess set to teach me how to play? I think it really is going to pay off." She looked at me, grinned, then looked at the board and moved her queen and exclaimed loudly, "Checkmate!"

Most of the lunch room turned to look at us. I looked down at the board and sure enough, she had got me. I congratulated her and tried to calm her down.

Maybe she was ready for Jamie after all!

14

Remembering Why

"I *really* missed you on Friday!" I said to Danielle as she sat on the swing next to me.

"I missed you too. I was over at Mary's house. They let me stay the night," she said, her feet leaving trails in the sand as she swayed back and forth. I was facing the woods and she was facing the back of the house.

"How's grandma been this weekend?" I probed, seeing if there was anything special I needed to know before talking to her.

"Same as usual I guess," she said with no effort.

"How's mama?" It came out bluntly. I don't know why I got a little nervous when asking the question. Not knowing where I stood with Sadie made me want to avoid it.

"She's been . . ." she looked up at me, looked at the house, and then looked at me again, "she's been doing okay I guess," she said, not very convincingly.

"What do you mean?"

"I really think mama still loves you. Do you know what's going to happen next? Are you going to do something to try and get back together?"

Now my feet were dragging in the sand. "Something's got to happen sometime sweetie; I'm just not sure when. But, remember what I said before, about daddy trying to do all I can to make it right?"

She nodded.

"I'm sticking to that promise," I said and got up and stood behind her and pushed her high. She laughed.

I stayed with her for a few more minutes at the swing set and then knew I had to talk to my mother before going to St. Joseph's. The swing slowed to a stop and I turned to face her, holding the chains.

"I'm going to go in and talk to grandma for a minute okay. You might want to stay out here," I said. She got the message and stood up and gave me a hug.

I put my hands on her shoulders and kissed her forehead and then she got back on the swing as I walked toward the house.

I got to the back screen door and looked inside. The kitchen was off to the left and straight ahead was the hall that ran down to the front door. I knocked.

She came from around the right corner—my parent's bedroom.

"Good morning Lewis," she said heading over to the sink, not looking at me.

"Do you mind if I come in for a minute?"

"Just for a minute. I've got to get breakfast cleaned up and then head to the store before lunch," she said, shuffling dishes and silverware off the counter.

The door squeaked open and shut again. I stood right inside, not wanting to intrude.

My plan was to be respectful, sincere, and to the point. "I just wanted to say that I was sorry for arguing with you in front of Mrs. Hannigan the other day. Regardless of how I felt, I still shouldn't have snapped at you like that."

She nodded, but was still messing with the dishes. I wasn't going to let it get to me.

"And also, it may not seem like it, but I *do* want and need your support. I don't know when or really how, but I'm going to try to work things out with Sadie. I just need you to believe in me," I said, trying to sound like a man and not a child. "Just like you said the other day, I need to do something about it. I just wanted to let you know that I keep intending to."

That's all I wanted to say. I was calm and there was a relief that entered me. She didn't look upset or angry or hurt. She stopped worrying about the plates and cups and put her hands on the counter and looked at me.

In an almost concerned, caring voice she asked, "Have you talked to Sadie yet?"

"No, I haven't. Hopefully it will be soon."

She nodded again and then went back to working at the sink. I waited, but she didn't say anything else. Finished, I walked through the house, through the main hallway and out the front door.

The scents of my past lingered on me as I headed toward the orphanage. I didn't know what I needed to do to help fix the relationship with my mother. But at the moment, as bad as it sounds, I didn't let it weigh on me. I had done my part and that was enough.

❖   ❖   ❖

It took everything I had in me to keep from literally running to Mr. Krueger's after I was done at St. Joseph's. Not until Dee asked, "How's work going?" did I remember what Mr. Krueger said, *'We've got a lot to talk about'*.

The bell rang above and I was elated to see that there were no customers looking to greet me. He was on the back aisle, re-pricing items.

"Afternoon Mr. Krueger," I said, trying to sound as upbeat as I could. It wasn't hard; I was feeling pretty good.

"Afternoon Lewis," he said, placing the price tags on some empty shelving. He looked me over and asked, "Are you feeling better?"

"I'm feeling much better sir!" I answered enthusiastically. "You said you wanted me here today feeling better because you had something you needed to talk to me about," I continued, searching for more information.

"And I do," he said. "Come with me."

I followed him as we walked back towards the front and then out the door. I hesitated, wondering if he wanted to keep the store unmanned, but he seemed to be okay with it. We walked a little to the right and turned around and faced backed toward the store. We were halfway in between his store and Taylor's Fashions next door.

He started talking as the midday sun shone down on us. "Keep this just between us if you don't mind, but Taylor's is going under. They've been having a hard time the last couple of years," he said, looking at the store. Then he looked at me, "to be honest, the hardware store has slid the last couple of years.

"But . . ." he continued, "I think there's an opportunity here that I'm going to take advantage of that can help the hardware store pick up a little more business and stay competitive for a few years longer."

"What are you thinking about?" My interest was piqued. I was trying to make the hardware store more personal. It was a part of me now, part of my responsibility and possibly part of my long-term stability. Whatever the future held for the store, the future possibly held for me, too.

"Well," he started, his hands pointing out to try and give a visual, "I would get the lease for the Taylor Place, cut out the wall in the middle to expand the hardware section and then use the other half of the new side for new products."

"New products?"

There was a small gleam in his eye—something I had never seen—as he said, "Krueger's Hardware and Home Appliance Center. What do you think?"

I smiled. It had a really good sound to it.

"As soon as I found out from Mr. Taylor a few months ago that he might be going under, I started thinking that we really don't have anywhere nearby that actually sells appliances: stoves, ovens, refrigerators and so on. Other than catalog sales you have to go nearly thirty miles to get them.

"I mean, Mr. Peterson down the block makes a good living repairing them, but he's never shown any interest in getting into retail."

I had never seen him like this. There was an energy that hadn't been there before. This is what he must have felt like when the hardware store first opened up. This is what he must have felt like in the picture.

"And that's why I need you," he said.

I turned from the building to look at him. For a moment, I had gotten so lost in his excitement that I forgot about me.

"I know it's only been a couple of weeks around the store, but you really have been doing a good job. And what's more Lewis, I feel like I can trust you. And if I'm going to do this venture I definitely can't do it on my own and as you've noticed, I don't have any other help.

"So," he said, turning to look at me, "will you stay on with me full time and help me get everything set up with the new store?"

"I appreciate the offer Mr. Krueger, I really do. I would love to stay on and help," I said, feeling excited.

"But there's only one thing," he added quickly.

There was a pause. He knew he was taking a chance on me and there was no way I could blow it. This was the best thing to happen to me on the way to getting Sadie back. Whatever he asked, I was willing to do it. I nodded.

"When this is all official—which should be sometime towards the middle of September, in about a month or so—I'm going to need you to act as my assistant manager and be in charge of the hardware store. There would be a raise, of course, not a lot, but it will be fair. Would you be willing to do that?"

I was stunned.

"Mr. Krueger, I don't . . . I don't know what to say. I'm honored, really I am. I've been trying to work hard and do my part. But I think . . ." I was trying not to stammer, but the words weren't coming, "but I think something like that might be a little . . . a little out of my league. Not only that, I just don't know if I . . . I'm just not sure if you want to . . ." I couldn't let it out. As much as he had done for me and as much as I wanted to accept his offer, I didn't want to let him down.

He brushed my stammering aside and by his expression I knew he knew what I was talking about.

"I'm not going to make you take on something you don't think you can handle. I just wanted you to know what was coming and that I wanted your help with it and that I have full faith that you will do a great job," he said firmly. "There are still a lot of things that have to fall into place before everything is finalized, so there's time for you to adjust and think about it and make sure *everything* is in place," he said, trying to reassure me.

There was a surge of confidence in me to hear him say that.

"Besides," he continued, "even if you're not *that good* it's better than having to train somebody all over again." A small, sarcastic grin came back to his face.

15

All of a Sudden

The next few days were a blur of energy and excitement. I truly felt like I had something to look forward to. All of a sudden, whenever I was at the hardware store I wanted to know and learn everything I could. I felt ownership, long after I hung up the apron.

Mom wasn't making her self openly available when I stopped by, so I didn't make any extra effort to say anything. I was tempted to tell her about the promotion, but I didn't want it to come across like I was trying to prove something. I just wanted us to have a relationship without having to worry and fret over each and every encounter. For now things were steady and that was enough.

Dee was actually the first person I told about the possible advancement at Mr. Krueger's store. She was so excited and happy that she actually gave me a hug. Even when she sat back down, she was still beaming.

I kept telling myself it was one more day until payday. Last week's five dollars seemed like such a large amount; this week's pay was going to feel like hitting the jackpot. There was nothing in particular I needed, but the idea of getting that money—to make it a habit—brought a sense of stability I needed.

There was a smile on my face as I stopped at the intersection of Maple and waited for a car to pass. I waited for it to drive by, looked both ways, and started to walk across the street. As soon as my feet touched the pavement I looked ahead.

My pulse started racing.

Sadie was walking in my direction carrying a bag of groceries. She still had not noticed me when I stepped up on the other side of the curb. The only thing I could do was stand there and wait.

My thoughts started turning. Maybe I should not let her see me? She said she didn't want to see me? What if I ruin it?

But it was completely by accident, regardless of how she took it. It was bound to happen sooner or later. As the seconds passed I was determined to make the most of it; completely beside myself at the anticipation of hearing her voice.

When her eyes found me she hesitated, but kept walking toward me. Looking at her I could tell this was a different Sadie than the one I talked to at the jail. Hopefully she would see that I was different, too.

Standing completely without thought, my only concern was that the meeting be positive, even a little.

When she reached me she stopped. With my hands in my pockets I asked, trying to sound casual, "Coming back from the market?"

"Yeah, Ms. Green needed a few extra things," she replied quietly. It was awkward.

People were passing by periodically. It was mid-afternoon and the crowds had started to arrive on Main Street for the days shopping. I continued, "How's Ms. Green's going?"

"It's fine."

A few seconds of silence passed with minimal eye contact, until she finally asked, "When was the last time you came by to see Danielle?"

"She didn't tell you?"

"We haven't really talked about it much."

"I stopped by the other day to see her. I've been able to get by and see her about twice a week or so. With my work and volunteer schedule, it's harder to catch the bus out to mom's house."

Sadie nodded. I could tell she was as nervous as I was. Her feet were having a hard time staying still.

"Lewis, I . . ." she started, but then stopped, frustrated.

She wanted to express something to me. Anything—some type of updated understanding on where she stood—I was willing to accept it.

"What is it Sadie? Anything at all, I just want you to know that . . ." and then I stopped. She had repositioned the grocery bag, moving it from one arm to another. It was just enough time for me to see what she couldn't say.

"Sadie?"

She finally looked me in the eyes, but didn't answer. A mixture of emotions were welling up inside of me.

"How long?" I asked mouth still half opened, stunned.

"About twenty-four weeks," she answered calmly. "I'm due at the end of November."

"But . . . ," I said, exhaling as I searched for the words. I felt betrayed, excited, and overwhelmed all at once. "Why didn't you tell me, or at least . . ."

She cut me off and said politely, but firmly, "I didn't tell you because I didn't want it to matter. I wanted to see . . ." she watched a few people pass by. She continued, her voice a little softer, "I . . . I just didn't want it to matter."

I just stood there and looked at her. Looking into her eyes I could see for the first time some hope; that I knew she wanted me to get straight. She was hoping that we would get back together.

The bag's weight finally gave in and she placed it gently on the sidewalk. The fingers on my right hand twitched a little as I felt the need to reach out and touch her hand as she bent back up. Isn't that what fathers-to-be did? Isn't that what husbands were supposed to do? But I restrained and said, "You know I've been trying to get myself straight so I could . . . so we could somehow make things right."

She looked down and nodded. After a brief pause she looked up and I could tell there was feeling inside of her. "How have things been going?"

"Things have been going real good and I've been doing the things I need to," I said, a feeling of peace settling inside me knowing I was telling the truth.

She had a small smile when she replied, "I'm glad to hear it." She glanced down at her watch and tensed up a bit. "I've uh . . . I've got to get going and get these back to Mrs. Green."

"Do you want some help?" I asked sincerely, wanting the moment to continue.

Her eyes caught mine and before the tears could form in hers she said, "That's alright, I got it." She wiped her eyes as she bent down to pick up the bag.

When she bent back up we were facing each other. I wanted to hold her, hug her—I wanted to be with her and let her sincerely know that I had changed.

Instinctively, I leaned in and kissed her on the cheek. She didn't flinch away. I looked at her and said, "I promise I'm changing and making it right. I want you to be able to trust me again."

She nodded and whispered, looking directly at me with sincere eyes, "I know, Lewis. I just still need some more time, okay." Then she smiled at me and started walking. I watched her walk away for a moment and then turned and headed to Krueger's knowing that what Judge Sanders had said was true; it was all about trust. I was determined that Sadie would be able to trust me again.

❖   ❖   ❖

After work, instead of heading home, I went to church. The same one I went to Bible Study at, the same one I got married in, the same one we would occasionally visit as a family.

The same church where my father was buried.

As I walked, my mind was jumping from Sadie, to a new baby, to Danielle, to assistant manager—to stability and to being a family again. With the surprise of seeing Sadie expecting and the feelings that were still there, I couldn't help but think that we were heading in the right direction. Even if I didn't have all the pieces together yet, it was a good feeling.

As I reached the church and made my way toward the cemetery the voice inside me that had eventually drowned out all other thoughts that afternoon—*'go talk to your father'*—finally began to fade. It didn't make any sense, but it didn't have to; it just felt right.

My feelings were the main reason I hadn't visited his grave since the funeral. I was ashamed. A simple look from him could cause me more grief and disappointment than any lecture ever would. I wanted to please him and prove my worth and there was no way for me to honestly stand over his remains . . . until now.

I opened the gate and made my way down the rows of headstones and markers. It was a modest cemetery, but well taken care of. There were hardly any trees or vegetation to add to the setting, just line after line of meticulously placed grassy pathways between the graves. The sun was still out though it was barely starting to fade. It was a gorgeous day and everything around me—the town, the cars, the people, nature – seemed still.

Without having to think about it I walked right to where he was buried. I wasn't sure what I would feel before coming, but *it* started to build as I stood over my father. As I put my hands in my pocket I started to shake a little on the inside and said the one thing I knew I needed to say, "I'm sorry I haven't come to visit."

When the words left my mouth and as the tears started to come the only thought that came to mind was the day I talked with Sadie in jail. That day I felt a huge weight, a heavy burden drop at my feet that I didn't want to deal with. As I stood with my dad, I felt that weight, that burden, lift from within me.

My body loosened and eased its way to the ground in front of his marker, tears still slowly, steadily falling. It was not loud or painful. It was peaceful.

> *Thomas "TJ" James Anderson*
> *Devoted Husband and Father*
> *1907-1953*

It wasn't enough. He was devoted, but there was so much more that needed to be said, that needed to be remembered. So much more that I had forgot to remember. Wiping my cheeks I looked around slowly. We were still alone.

I took in a deep breath and exhaled. It wasn't his fault. I was ready to let it go, let him go. I was ready to move on. It felt as if everything was coming into line and making sense. I didn't see any visions or hear any voices. As I sat there on the ground the last piece of the puzzle was put into place and I was ready to see the whole picture.

I was ready to be a man. I was ready to be like him.

After that, I just talked. I've never considered myself overly religious, but I felt like he could hear me. It doesn't matter whether or not it's true, at the time that's what I needed. In a way, I guess that makes it true regardless.

I told him how Danielle was getting so tall and excited about school and her birthday coming up. She was my pride and joy and was being so strong. I talked about Sadie and how I loved her and understood why she decided not to tell me about the baby and how I couldn't believe I was going to be a dad again. Then there was the prospect of a full-time job at the hardware store and how much I thought him and Mr. Krueger would have really liked each other. Then I thought about mama and I could feel the emotion coming back.

All this time the one thing I was too selfish to do was look at her like he did. I couldn't bring myself to say out loud how things were going between us, even though they seemed to be improving, slowly. I wasn't ready. He probably knew anyway. Hopefully he understood.

When I ran out of things to say I just sat, feeling the breeze blow, and waited for the night to fall. As it did, and the day started slipping, I told him goodbye and promised him I'd be back. I eventually stood to leave. Before turning to head back out the gated entrance, I remembered one more thing I needed to do, and smiled.

"Dee wanted me to say thank you for the chess set."

16

Long Enough

"She can't get any more madder at you, can she?" Dee asked as she moved her pawn out to start the match. "It just seems like it was supposed to happen. You were *meant* to run into each other." For the past three days her voice had been more serious, more prodding than usual...

'*You should go see her.*'

I knew it was the next step, but I didn't know when. Friday, the day after I saw her, would have been too desperate. Saturday, I ended up working more than my usual shift at the store and was there all day. The temptation was there to go to mom's house on the way home, even though it was late. Sadie would have almost certainly been there, but my feet wouldn't make the turn down Thurman Street.

I moved my knight out into play. Dee was glaring at me, waiting for a response.

"It's not going to be that easy. The timing has to be right."

"Oh you're just being a chicken," she said sharply, impatiently. Normally, there would have been some playfulness in her voice, but she meant it. I took offense.

"Now just wait . . . she's put this whole thing on her terms and it's getting better, I'll admit that, but the timing still has to be right. I just can't show up after one visit and expect everything to be all better."

Stubbornly, she was looking at the board, hand on her bishop. She had completely ignored me.

"I still say that you are stupid if you don't go and see her tonight." The edge in her voice faded and there was more emotion. A few seconds passed and then she looked up at me and spoke from a place I had not yet seen, "Every day you wait is another day Danielle doesn't have a daddy."

I looked back down at the board and realized we both didn't care about the game. For the moment, I was thinking in terms of Sadie. But the conversation and the subsequent outcome was on a whole different level for Dee. Though she probably understood more than most her age about relationships and adulthood, what she knew best was being a little girl. All she cared about was Danielle.

We had never broached the subject and on impulse I couldn't help but ask. "Do you still think about them?"

She pulled her bear a little closer, "Yeah, pretty much every day."

"How much do you remember?" I asked, crossing the line, but not caring. She looked at me and with her silence answered my question. She remembered more than she was willing to share. She only had shared what was needed. I didn't press her for any more.

"Do you ever get mad or upset, you know, having to be on your own? Not having your parents to be here with you?" As with the first question, it was wrong of me to ask, but I couldn't hold it back.

As she continued to look directly into my eyes, she said, "Does Danielle ever get mad at you?"

We both knew the answer. As the unconditional truth of her statement set in I shook my head and simply said, "No."

All she did was nod and say, "That's why you can't wait."

I nodded back.

Without even thinking I started pushing the chess pieces away. Dee didn't seem to mind, but sat and watched. When I was finished I handed her the box and she stood. As I reached out for her shoulder, I knelt down, and pulled her close for a hug. It was quick, sincere, and heartfelt.

"You're a very special young lady," I said as I stood and backed up.

"Thanks Lewis, you're not so bad yourself!" she said as she started making her way over to her table just as the bell rang.

I watched her walk away, cleared off my table, finished in the kitchen, and walked out the back door trying to figure out what I would say when I went to see my wife and daughter.

❖   ❖   ❖

It was pitch black by the time I made it to my mother's house. After I left the orphanage, I spent the better part of the afternoon pacing the confines of my house plotting, speculating the best way to approach the moment. The only thing I knew was that it should be dark; something about the mood being calmer and the day having wound down that just seemed right. But the rest of the scenario wasn't as concrete.

Walking up the driveway, after too much time to think about it, I was to the point of just wanting it to be over. I wanted to know where I stood, almost regardless of the outcome.

Almost.

A few of the lights were on in the house, but I couldn't see anybody. I made it up to the porch without being noticed. With as nice as the weather was it was unusual for the door and the screen to both be closed.

I paused at the bottom of the steps and took in a deep breath. This was it. There was no turning back. The time for worrying or uncertainty had faded. Dee was right, '*every day I wait . . .* '

I knocked on the door. Footsteps were coming and I was expecting my mother, but the front porch light turned on and Sadie opened the door. I didn't say anything and she hesitated before opening the screen door and coming all the way out on the porch. The door shut behind her and I stepped back to give her some room. She gathered her thoughts and I didn't rush her.

"Hi, Lewis," she said softly, patiently. She wasn't noticeably angry. "What do you want?" She knew the answer, but probably didn't know what else to say.

"I just wanted to talk. I just . . . just wanted to pick up where we left off," I said. She looked up at me. "Pick up where we left off on the street the other day. I thought it was."

She didn't respond, but turned to sit down in the nearby rocking chair. I tried to catch a glimpse of her stomach, but her clothes were too relaxed, too loose for me to see anything.

"How has the pregnancy been?" I asked sincerely. Danielle had been especially hard on her with morning sickness.

Putting her hand on her stomach she said, "Actually, not that bad. It was rough at the beginning, but it's gotten better as the weeks have gone on. He's been kicking lately."

"It's a boy?" I said excitedly, forgetting the tension that we were supposed to be feeling.

"I don't know for sure of course, but that's what Danielle thinks," she said.

I nodded. A son. It had always just been the three of us— a boy sounded right.

"Mr. Krueger offered me an assistant manager position at the hardware store. He's going to be expanding next month," I said.

"Do you like it there?"

"Yeah, I do. Mr. Krueger is a very nice man and has really given me an opportunity. So far, it's been going great. He has really good ideas and I think I can help."

For the first time in almost two months she seemed relaxed and said, "It's been a long time since I've really seen you smile."

I didn't answer and there was another long pause.

"So do you think it will be a long term position?"

"I do. He's been at that place forever and has steady business and what he's planning should help bring more business." We were actually having a conversation on my mother's front porch. If I wasn't sitting there doing half the talking I wouldn't have believed it.

"Is Danielle excited about her birthday?" I continued. It was coming up in a couple of weeks.

"Yeah, she is," was all she could say.

Sadie turned her head toward the front door. There was a movement on the inside as if someone was backing away down the hall.

"Danielle?" I asked.

"Probably," she said, smiling.

"It's been a long time since I've really seen you smile, too," I said, trying to feed off the positive vibe of the conversation.

"Are we heading in the right direction? I mean, are we back on track to . . . to being a family again?" I heard the words coming out of my mouth before I could stop them.

Her smile went away and was replaced with an expression that was simpler, softer. It wasn't anger or frustration, but honesty.

"I think so. I'm not ready—I don't think yet. But I'm ready . . . I'm ready to work on it, whatever that means," she said quietly, looking at me. "I really am proud of you Lewis and I want to trust you," she added. I was looking back at her and smiled again. It was more than I could have hoped for.

"I know you do," I said. I walked over closer to her and put my hand on her shoulder. "Thanks for being patient."

She put her hand up on mine and looked up at me. "I love you. Just keep it together and keep doing what you've been doing."

"Can I come see Danielle *and* you?"

"I think that would be fine," she said letting go of my hand and getting up from the rocking chair. We stood in front of each other, more intimately than we had in a very long time.

Before I could do anything she leaned in and placed a small, simple kiss on my lips. I kept my hands by my side, but kissed back. It was soft, tender.

"Good night," she said as she walked pass me and back into the house. I stood on the porch, the light shining off my right cheek as the door closed behind her. Waiting on the steps for a few seconds, I tried to process all that had just happened.

113

Eventually, I walked off the porch with my adrenaline pumping so fast I felt like I could run through a brick wall.

17

The Proposition

"Do you ever stop smiling Lewis?" Mr. Krueger asked as I walked into the store. With the way my life had gone the previous ten days, the definite answer was . . .

"No, not lately!" I said with enthusiasm. And though the hardware store continued to bring encouragement and promise, it was not the main reason for my joy.

"How did it go last night with Sadie?"

"It went really good Mr. Krueger—really good," I answered, coming out from the back room with my apron on. A relationship with him was starting to form. Working side by side, day after day, was bringing a bond.

Since going over to my mother's house and talking with Sadie on the porch, we had continued to take small steps. All signs were pointing to us getting back together.

The key was that we were talking and working things out. The 'last night' Mr. Krueger referred to was an actual date; the first one we had been on in a very, very long time. When I went to pick Sadie up, Danielle was waiting on the porch. She was the happiest I had ever seen her.

She gave me a big hug as we met on the steps. I was coming to visit so often that there wasn't anymore jumping and yelling when she saw me.

"Are you going out with mom?"

"Yes ma'am!" I said, tweaking her nose. She laughed.

"I think she's real excited. She's been standing in front of the mirror since she got home from work trying on dresses," she said, changing her position back and forth to pretend like she was posing.

As I laughed with Danielle the front door opened and Sadie came out. I never considered myself overly attentive in regards to my wife's wardrobe, but the dress she was wearing seemed new. She was beautiful.

Sadie looked knowingly at Danielle and her pretend mirror. Danielle tried to play it off, but with no luck. We all started laughing.

"I'll see you on Thursday," I said to Danielle, referring to her birthday party.

"Make sure you bring me something *big*," she said, holding her hands out. Sadie had mentioned a new bike was on the top of the list.

The rest of the night went great. Sadie and I talked, laughed, and enjoyed each other's company. We walked and got something to eat and walked some more. She was letting her guard down and letting me in.

The bell above the door rang as another customer came in.

"I'm really happy for you Lewis," Mr. Krueger said.

"Thank you, sir, I really appreciate it. Well, I'm going to get back to the back and get ready for the shipment tomorrow. Do you need anything?"

"No Lewis, that should be fine," he answered.

Each week was becoming easier and easier. As I became familiar with the surroundings and created my own system, it helped to keep everything organized. Mr. Krueger had basically given me full run of the back area, allowing me to try things out and rearrange as I felt necessary. The only stipulation that remained in effect was that I was not to touch his papers or binders on the bookkeeper's desk.

116

It was well into the afternoon when I saw Mr. Krueger again. He stuck his head through the curtain. I put down the boxes of nails I was holding and wiped my forehead off.

"Can you come out front for a minute Lewis?"

I didn't respond but followed him through the curtain. I continued to wipe off my arms and around the back of my neck as we walked.

When we got towards the front he said, "Here he is." As he moved behind the register I finally paid attention to who he was talking too.

"Sadie?" She was standing in front of the register. I looked at her and then at Mr. Krueger. He was trying to be unobtrusive and was appearing to ruffle through some papers. There was a slight grin on his face.

"I'm really sorry to come see you at work Lewis. There was just something I really wanted to talk to you about and was hoping you might have a couple of minutes," she said, looking at Mr. Krueger.

He didn't say a word but nodded his head, giving permission. I motioned for Sadie to go through the front door. She opened it and we stood next to each other on the sidewalk.

"What's the matter? Is everything okay?"

"Yeah, everything's okay, I just needed to talk to you today. I've been doing a lot of thinking. After last night . . ." she hesitated as some people walked by. "I really had a good time last night. And this last week has been really good for us. You seem really happy and it seems like things are coming together."

I took her by the hand. "I can honestly say I'm where I need to be. I feel good about everything: about work, about the drinking, about us."

She picked up at the end of my sentence, having thought about what she wanted to say, "There's one thing I haven't heard you talk about. What about . . . what about your dad? Have you dealt with it? I mean are you okay with it now?" she asked.

"Yeah, I have," I answered, honestly.

There was relief in her face. She knew I was sincere and wasn't just telling her what she wanted to hear.

117

She nodded and continued. "Then I think that we shouldn't get Danielle a bike for her birthday."

My expression changed noticeably. "Uh, okay." I wasn't sure where to go with the sudden topic change. "But what does that have . . ."

"I have something to give her that she would appreciate a lot more than a bike, I think," she interrupted, smiling. I just stood there, waiting for the punch line.

She moved in closer and took both my hands. "I think tomorrow for her birthday we should tell her that we're ready to move back in together. All of us, living together again, back in the same house."

It took a few seconds for it to sink in, but when it did, I screamed. I couldn't help it. I picked her up and spun her around and we kissed. Well, it wasn't much of a kiss—I was yelling and she was laughing—but it was a special embrace.

When I finally put her down, I didn't know where to start, but she filled me in on how it might work. We would tell Danielle after her party; just us together as a family. Then if Mr. Krueger was willing to give me the afternoon off we would move everything the next day after I was done at St. Joseph's.

"I'll talk to Mr. Krueger, but I think he'll be okay with it," I said, still beaming. "Are you sure?"

"I'm sure, Lewis. I'm ready," she said reassuringly.

I gave her a hug and we looked at each other.

"You better get back to work."

"I'll see you tomorrow," I said, pulling her close again to hold her.

I had done it.

She left me and I went back inside. Mr. Krueger was still at the register. There were no customer's in the store.

"So," he started, giving me a knowing grin, "how did that go?"

"Did she already talk to you?"

His grin turned into a full smile. "Yes. We talked for a few minutes before I came and pulled you from the back." Before I could even ask, he continued, "I think it sounds like a great idea and I should be able to manage by myself on

118

Friday. You've got a family to take care of," he said and went back to working at the register.

18

Gratitude

"So did you win?" I asked Dee as soon as she was in voice range. By the look on her face I already knew the answer. "How bad was it?" I continued.

"It wasn't horrible," she responded, sitting down. "He didn't cream me or anything. I guess I just got my hopes up."

"That's too bad. But at least you proved him wrong, huh?" I said, trying to be positive. "Girls *can* play chess!"

"You're right. And it was nice of you to show me how to play. Really, I appreciate it," she said sitting down. It was the first day in a few weeks that there wasn't a chess board in front of us. "It's just now he has something else to rub in. He was unbearable enough before."

"I'm proud of you regardless," I replied.

She finally smiled that big, wide smile. It was good to see her smile because I wasn't sure how to broach the subject we needed to talk about. I tried to ease into it.

"Dee, I don't think we've really talked about it lately, but do you remember the first few days I was here and you asked how long I would be volunteering for?"

"Yes, you said a month. You don't have to sugar coat it Lewis, I know it's coming up soon," she said flatly, her expression lowered again.

I couldn't do it! How was I supposed to tell her that not only was I done coming everyday but that my family was together and happy again? What joy could that possibly bring her? I know she cared for me and my family, but how could I expect her to be that unselfish.

But, I felt I owed it to her; she had given me so much support. She would want to know.

"My last day is going to be this Sunday. I'll be here tomorrow, then after that I'm helping my wife and daughter move back in with me, then I'll be at Krueger's all day Saturday and then on Sun . . ."

"What did you say?" she asked, eyes squinted, transfixed on me.

"I said my last day is going to be this Sunday?"

"No—what about your family? Are you guys getting back together, is that what you said?"

"Yes, we're telling Danielle today for her birthday and then we're moving tomorrow back into our house."

"Lewis that is fantastic!" she bellowed at the top of her lungs. The whole lunchroom turned to look and Sister Meredith started walking over. She didn't look at me, but went straight after Dee. She wasn't happy.

Dee quickly folded her arms and pursed her lips, as if ready for inspection.

"Dee, that was uncalled for young lady! Mr. Anderson is trying to eat his lunch in peace. I am so sorry for the outburst Mr. Anderson," she said.

"It's really okay Sister Meredith, really. Dee was just surprised about something. It won't happen again, will it Dee?" I asked, eyebrows raised.

Holding in her laughter through her pursed lips she shook her head. I could tell Sister Meredith didn't buy the routine, but she went back to her table anyway. Dee let out a giggle and then came back to the subject at hand.

"I'm so excited for you Lewis. That is great!" She meant every word of it. I sat there, staring at her, amazed, not sure what to think. Dee had been an encouragement to me, a friend to me and I know she wanted to see my family together; but given her circumstances I didn't expect excitement.

"I'm sorry Dee," I said in a moment of pity.

"Sorry for what?" she asked, still half beaming, but a little confused.

"I just . . . it's just that I feel like I'm abandoning you here, that's all," was the safest answer I could come up with. It was true.

"Oh no you're not," she said, waving it off. "Please don't feel bad for me Lewis. That's the last thing I need is people feeling bad for me. It's not like you're leaving forever."

I couldn't tell if it was a statement or a question.

"Even though I'm done with my service I'll definitely come back to visit. I'm excited for Danielle to meet you. You two will really like each other," I said, reassuring her.

"I look forward to it. And hey," she said, her eyes getting excited again, "maybe I can teach her how to play chess. Does she know how?"

"Nope, not yet. That sounds like a real good idea."

The bell rang to end lunch. Dee grabbed Reginald and gave me a hug.

"Thank you," she said into my ear before she walked toward the exit. I felt as if her words were a substitute for something deeper, but humbly accepted what she was willing to give.

❖   ❖   ❖

I practically sprinted down Main Street. The hardware store required a certain amount of physical labor, but nothing as intensive as running. By the time I reached the courthouse I felt as if I had to vomit and pass out, respectively.

Skipping as many steps as I could I hurriedly made it into the corridor before the closing time of six o'clock. If my burst of recreation had not been in vain, I would be rewarded with seeing Judge Sanders.

My heart was beating rapidly. But this time, it wasn't because I needed to confess. This visit was solely about showing gratitude. I don't know why I ran; standing there sweaty and out of breath I felt silly. There was no emergency. I just needed to talk to him before Danielle's party and tell him thank you.

"Yes sir, how might I help you?" Betty asked, alarmed, as I ran up full speed and then suddenly stopped at the front of her desk. Completely out of breath and gasping for air I put my hands on my hips and bent over.

"Are you okay sir?"

I nodded and inhaled deeply. "Is Judge . . . Sanders . . . still in?" I finally got out.

"I'll see if he's free. What's your name sir?"

"Lewis," I said and paused to take another deep breath. "Lewis Anderson."

She got up, knocked on the door behind her and walked in. I leaned up against the desk, still trying to restore my lungs to normalness. Judge Sander's door opened.

"You can come in Mr. Anderson," she said politely and let me pass.

He was walking towards the door as I came in. "Well this is quite a surprise Lewis. What brings you around so late in the day?" he asked. It was the first time we had talked since his backyard. As much as I looked up to him and respected him, I didn't think it appropriate to give him ongoing details of how I had been doing.

"I've got really good news—Sadie and I are back together. She and my daughter are moving back in tomorrow. I wanted to come and tell you myself and to say . . . well . . . to just tell you how much I appreciate all that you've done for me," I said, breathing heavily.

There was a smile on his face as he put both hands on my shoulders. "Lewis, all I can say is that I am happy for you and your family. If our meeting had to come in the way it did, then I will consider it a blessing for both of us." If that's how he wanted to accept my appreciation I was okay with it. From his body language I could tell he wasn't comfortable with the praise I was trying to shower on him, so I decided to keep it brief.

We talked for a few more minutes about the orphanage and about Krueger's and how on track everything seemed to be going. I talked about the prospect of expanding the new store and how I had been dry for almost three weeks, with no desire to drink.

All he did was smile and nod, he was sincere, but uncomfortable I could tell. What had happened between us would stay between us. He did it out of a sincere desire to help, nothing more.

"I won't keep you any longer Judge Sanders, I just really wanted to say thank you. Do you mind if sometime in the near future I bring my family up here to say hi? It would really mean a lot to me," I asked.

"I think that would be okay, Lewis. Usually later in the afternoon is better. By then I'm out of court," he said as we walked back toward the door. He opened it and we stood there, waiting.

I stuck out my hand and he took it. "Congratulations Lewis."

"Thank you," I replied and turned to go. "Oh, there's one thing I forgot. I forgot to tell you that I'm . . ."

He cut me off. "I know about that too and I hope it's a little boy. Have a good day," he said as he closed the door.

I stood there, next to the secretary's desk, baffled. Involuntarily, I looked over at Betty. She smiled knowingly as she returned my glance and whispered, "He makes it his job to *always* know *everything*."

As I left I was grateful that he cared enough to want to know anything at all.

19

_____

Daddies, Daughters, and Teddy Bears

Danielle knew something was up when she didn't get a present from us. She hid it pretty well until all of her friends were gone. When the door closed behind the last guest she asked in a very upbeat, hopeful manner "Is there something *else* for me?"

We looked at each other and tried to play it off. I shrugged my shoulders and said, "I think Grandma might have something for you when she gets back from Mrs. Hannigan's."

My mother was in hiding. It's not that she didn't want to support Danielle on her birthday; she just didn't want to be around all the 'rambunctious' kids. Sadie had already talked to her about the move and so far it had been hard to pick up a reading. Did she think we were ready? Did she think I could stay on top of things? At the time it didn't matter—Sadie and I were still moving forward—but I was hoping for some positive support.

After dragging Danielle along most of the night we finally broke down and told her. She cried. We all cried. I made a lot of promises to them as we sat huddled together on the couch.

"I'll get to see you everyday now, huh?" she asked.

"Yes."

"Everything's all better?"

I nodded, "Everything's all better."

"I'm gonna start packing!" she said excitedly as she jumped up and ran into the bedroom. Sadie and I smiled at each other and moved closer together. She was leaning in on my chest.

"Why don't you two come with me on Sunday to St. Joseph's? I think you would enjoy it. It's my last official day there and I would like for you to meet a couple of people," I said.

"Who?" she said looking up at me.

"Well, Ms. Weston, the head lady there is really nice; I think you would really like her. And then one of the girls there that I've gotten to know, I think her and Danielle would hit if off really well."

Sadie responded apprehensively, "Not to ruin your plans but I had hoped to take the whole weekend to get the house straight. There is quite a bit that has to be done. I would love to meet them, really I would, but can it be some other time?"

"Yeah, there is a lot to do. I understand. There will be plenty of other visits we can make," I said, disappointed.

"You could still take Danielle if she wants to go. She would like that; just to get out with you for a while."

"I'll ask her when she gets done packing," I said. I really wanted all of us to go, as a family, but it wasn't time to push anything with Sadie. I would take my daughter and enjoy the time we had together, just us two.

❖   ❖   ❖

"Come on sweetie, we have to go. I can't be late!" I said to Danielle through the bathroom door. There couldn't have been a happier man on the earth to have his wife and

128

daughter back together with him, but there were still some practical issues we were working on. Bathroom time was one of them.

"I'm coming, jeesh," she replied impatiently.

I looked down the hall at Sadie who was walking towards me. "When did she grow up?"

She just shook her head and said, "Welcome home."

Little intricacies aside it was great to be home—to have a place to call home again. The move went fine the day after the party. There really wasn't much to move, mostly clothes and odds and ends. The only heavy stuff was a dresser and a nightstand. They didn't completely fit in the trunk of my mother's car, but it did the trick.

I probably didn't have to take the whole day off from Mr. Krueger's, but it was nice to have the flexibility. We took our time and enjoyed the moment. It was a starting over for all of us and it was good not to have to rush. Sadie and Danielle went to the store in the afternoon for groceries and we all helped prepare dinner that night. We ate dinner together around the table. It was simple and quiet. It was perfect.

"What are you going to do while we're gone?" I asked Sadie. She looked around the house. Everything was pretty well in order.

"Rest," she said happily.

"We should be back by two or so," I said as I leaned in and gave her a kiss.

"I love you," she said.

"I love you, too."

There was a knock at the door and we looked at each other, not expecting anybody. I went to the door and opened it—it was my mother. I stood there, silent. She was the last person I had expected to see. She was holding a bag in her hand and a lamp was lying next to her on the porch.

"I just thought I would stop by on my way over to Ruth's and drop off some stuff that Danielle left. I know it's not anything of major importance, but I thought she would want it," she said, extending the bag for me to take.

"Well, that was very kind of you mom, but you know you didn't have to do that. We would have eventually gotten it," I said, still taken at the sight of seeing her at my—our—front door.

She was not interested in niceties. "It really isn't a big deal. Just wanted to help," she said, handing me the lamp. "Tell Danielle and Sadie I said hi."

I took the lamp from her and before she could turn and go down the porch I said, "Mom, it would be nice if you came for dinner some time."

"We'll see," she answered, heading down the steps facing the street. I stood there holding the bag, smiling, knowing that there was still a long way to go, but thankful we were heading in the right direction.

When the door closed behind me and the bag and the lamp were safe inside, Sadie said, "It's just how she is—you know that, right?"

"I know," I said, smiling to myself, remembering I needed to try and see her like my father did. I just needed to take it one day at a time and move in a positive direction.

The bathroom door opened up.

"Finally!" I said, somewhat dramatically.

Danielle hit me in the elbow. I put my arm around her shoulder and we walked out the door and headed to St. Joseph's.

❖   ❖   ❖

"Wow, it's really big!" she said when she first saw St. Joseph's. "Are they having church in there today, too?"

"I think they probably already had it and are getting ready for lunch."

I was about thirty minutes late. It's not that I wanted to leave a bad impression on my last day—the time with my daughter at that moment was more important. I hoped Ms. Weston would understand. I honestly didn't care what Sister Catherine thought.

As we reached the main entrance, Danielle's tone got more somber. "Daddy," she said stopping at the fountain, looking up at the massive structure, "what happened to the boys and girls in here." She didn't quite understand.

"They are orphans sweetie. That means that their mom's and dad's are . . . are . . . gone. The kids come here and the sisters take care of them until they can find other parents that will love and take care of them. Does that make sense?" I asked, trying not to be too specific.

She nodded. "How old are they? Are there babies?"

"Yeah, there are a couple of babies, but mostly boys and girls around your age."

"Okay," she said contentedly and we made our way to the double doors. When I opened them and we stepped into the foyer she said, out of the blue, "You and mom are going to keep Jacob, right?"

The door closed with a thud and we stood alone in the vaulted foyer. There was an organ piping in the chapel.

"What?" I asked. "Who's Jacob?"

"The new baby—Jacob. We're going to keep him right? I mean, we don't need to give him away, do we?" she asked genuinely. Sadie had said Danielle thought we might have a boy.

Jacob.

"So if it's a boy you think Jacob is a good name, huh?" I asked, getting lost in my own thoughts of the idea of having another baby.

I smiled and answered, "Of course we're going to keep him honey. We have no reason to want to give him up. Are you excited to have a little baby in the house?" I asked as I led her to the right, down the administrative hallway.

"As long as he doesn't cry *too* much," she answered. I laughed as we kept walking.

"You'll like Ms. Weston, she's a real nice lady," I said as we walked to the end of the hall into the back office. As expected, Sister Maria was sitting at her desk.

She looked up and saw me; there was worry and uncertainty in her eyes. Before she could say anything I looked into Ms. Weston's office and saw her sitting in her chair, looking out the window at the playground. She seemed extremely tense and troubled.

"Ms. Weston, what's wrong?" I asked.

"Dee ran away," she said, turning her chair around. She was holding Reginald in her lap.

131

I didn't believe her.

"Ms. Weston, I don't think Dee would have run away. You might not be able to find her right now, but . . . but to think that she up and ran away . . ."

She reached on her desk and handed me a piece of paper. "When the sisters went to wake the girls up this morning all they found was her bear and this note. We've questioned all the girls multiple times and I'm very certain it's not a game. You were probably closer to her than anyone in here; did she ever give you any reason why she might run away? Was she upset or depressed about something? Anything?" she asked, searching for some clue.

I opened the note and read.

Thank you for all your love and help.
Things have changed and it is time for me to go.
Please leave Reginald with Lewis - he'll know what to do with him.

Love,

Dee

I read the note again and then looked up at Ms. Weston. "I'll know what to do with him? What does that mean? How could she run away? Where would she go?" I wanted to do something, but I didn't know what.

Ms. Weston just shook her head. "I don't know Mr. Anderson. I was hoping you might know. We did an initial search of the grounds this morning and we are fairly positive she's not here. As soon as we realized she was gone I called the police."

Danielle grabbed a hold of my forearm. Runaway. Police. She understood enough of the conversation to know it wasn't good.

"Can we go out and look for her; I mean people from here or the community?" I asked.

"The police said that anything we do would be helpful, but it's not like the staff here can just up and leave the other children. As far as the community, the police will put up signs and alert the bus depots, but other than that there's not much we can do—other than hope and pray that she's safe and will come back."

I pulled Danielle to me and nodded. "Is there anything I can do?"

"Just let us know if you hear anything and keep an eye out. Really Lewis," Ms. Weston continued in a reassuring voice, "you have done so much and made a big difference. I'm sure she's okay. Maybe she just needed to get away for a while." Her face didn't seem to show the same hope.

Maybe she ran away because she was mad at me? Maybe she was upset for getting my family back together? If nothing else, after all that time, I felt that we had bonded. I felt like I had built a relationship with her; one of trust. It didn't make any sense.

"This must be your daughter, Lewis. I'm sorry you had to come today when everything's so hectic," she said, extending a warm hand to Danielle. Danielle hesitated, but put out her hand and they shook. "Are you sure we haven't met before Miss Anderson?" she asked, looking at Danielle enquiringly.

"No," I answered, "this is the first time she's been here." Danielle remained silent, still unsure of the situation. "I just wish there was something I could do Ms. Weston."

"Me too, Lewis."

Danielle squeezed my hand and I looked at her. She didn't want to be there anymore.

"Well, please let me know if you hear anything. Do you have my number?" I asked.

"Yes. I apologize for not calling you earlier, but by the time I had a free moment I figured you were on your way."

"It's okay, I understand. Thank you again for everything Ms. Weston."

"Thank you, too. And for today, don't worry about the cafeteria. Given the circumstances, I think it's okay if you miss your last day," she said, "and don't forget to take the bear. She left it specifically for you."

As soon as I grabbed him and felt his soft fur in my hand I couldn't help but think that I had failed Dee in some way. If Dee had actually run away, then I couldn't help but feel that my time at the orphanage had been a waste.

"Come on sweetie, it's time to go," I said to Danielle, taking hold of her hand. She followed me without hesitating.

I held on to Reginald as we made our way out of the office up the hallway and out the front doors. I wanted to do something.

There was silence as we walked past the fountain, down the drive and back up Franklin toward Main Street to catch the bus back home. Every few steps Danielle would look up at me and then look back down the street. I didn't know what to say to her.

When we got to the bus stop we stood close to each other and waited. The bench was already occupied by an older woman with a large hand bag.

After a few minutes Danielle tapped me on the elbow. "Daddy, do you think I could hold the teddy bear some?" To be honest, I had forgotten that I was still holding him.

"Sure baby," I answered, giving him to her.

Eventually the bus came and we got on. It wasn't very full so we found a secluded spot toward the back. Danielle sat next to the window and seemed content with Reginald. That was good; I needed some time to try and clear my thoughts.

Involuntarily I scanned the bus. There was what appeared to be a church couple heading home from the days services in the front; a few teenagers in the middle heading back from downtown; and the older woman with the handbag was sitting in the very back seat. She had pulled some yarn out and was knitting.

"Dad, what was the girl's name that ran away?" Danielle asked.

"It was Dee," I answered, gazing out the window.

"Then why is my name already on the bear?" she asked.

It took a second for her words to register and then I looked over. She was holding Reginald by one of his legs and on his paw I could see the small handwritten 'D' I had seen before, followed by 'ANIELLE'.

Had Dee written it on there? Dee . . .

I turned back around to look at the lady at the back of the bus that was knitting.

'He'll know what to do with him?'

"Let daddy see him for a minute," I said. I picked Reginald up and moved his knitted scarf over to the side. With my fingers pinched I reached into Reginald. Danielle looked at me strangely, wondering why I was torturing a poor, defenceless stuffed animal. "It's okay; I promise."

When I felt the piece of paper in between my fingers there was a surge of hope inside me. Dee would tell me where she went. We could find her and she would be safe.

Danielle asked curiously, "What is it dad?"

"It's a letter from Dee." Danielle was speechless. I unfolded it and started reading. It *was* a letter from Dee.

Dear Lewis,

First of all, I just want you to know that I will be okay and that I will miss you. This might not all make sense at first, but if you go with your heart, it doesn't have to. If you never stop believing in miracles, they will never stop coming true. Consider our time together a small miracle!

Second, I wanted to tell you how happy I am for you being able to get back together with your family. I was sent to St. Joseph's for a reason - you. The timing wasn't coincidence. I was sent to help in whatever small way I could. I was sent to help you see what unfortunately would have been if you would have kept going down the road you were on. It's been my experience that people have a hard time seeing just how much their decisions in life really affect others. Thankfully, you saw what you would lose and made the choice to go down a different path.

Third, thank you so much for all the lunch time conversation and teaching me how to play chess – I know it took a lot of patience. I really had a lot of fun. Your dad said you had a good heart and he was right (and he agrees with Danielle that Jacob is a good name for a boy – I agree)!

It's time for me to move on, but know that I will think of you often!

Love,

Dee

PS – Sorry I wasn't able to stick around to show Danielle how to play chess, but to be honest, I think that's something that dad's are better at teaching anyway!

I read the letter again and my spine tingled. My mind was arguing with my heart that what I was reading wasn't true. How could it be?

Yet it was, I felt it. She was right, it didn't make sense. But I felt it. I read the third paragraph again and I felt it even stronger and had to wipe my eyes. It didn't make any sense. A lot of things in life don't make sense, and don't have to; they just have to feel right and be acted upon.

At that moment I knew that I would never see the little girl from the orphanage again. According to the letter, according to Dee, that was a good thing. I knew from the choices I had made that it was true.

"What's wrong dad?" Danielle asked, noticing my tears.

I wiped my eyes again and instinctively handed Reginald back to her. I put my arm gently around her shoulder and pulled her to me and kissed her forehead.

"I'm okay," I said. "I think Dee would want you to have him. Consider it a late birthday present."

"Do you think so?" she said, puzzled. "What if she comes back?"

"I don't think she's coming back," I said calmly, looking down at Reginald and then back at her, "she doesn't need to."

She was pleased enough with the response and held him close again. Everything was going to be okay. I still didn't understand it, but I knew that everything was going to be okay.

Danielle looked at me and smiled. I smiled back and said, "Would you mind if I teach you how to play chess sometime?"

She thought for a moment, "Isn't that the game that you and grandpa used to play?"

"Yes baby, it is."

Endnote

The book that you now hold in your hands came into my possession roughly five years ago. Lewis left it to me as a manuscript and asked me to share it with 'the world' for him. I'm not sure about getting it out to 'the world', but the fact that you are reading it would bring him some satisfaction.

This is only a part of Lewis's story; it is by no means the complete story. I thought you might like to know what happened next. I can see why Lewis ended the story where he did—it was his turning point. Once he made the decision, once he made the greatest choice if you will, his life was on a solid footing. Granted he had bumps in the road, as we all do, but he was pretty much heading in the right direction.

Because of all that Lewis did for me, to say that I was intrigued with him and his life is an understatement. I was able to piece together pretty much the major details of his life. It shows how he transformed from an unsure, unsteady young man trying to get his life back on track to the wise, mature mentor that gently guided me all those many hours in a secluded library room.

He got back together with Sadie and they moved into his grandparent's old house. The following month Mr. Krueger did end up getting the storefront next door and turned it into an appliance center and it was very successful. Then the following month Sadie delivered a healthy baby boy and they named him Jacob.

Lewis became assistant manager in charge of the hardware store and from there his career slowly took off. He worked at the store for ten years until the chain stores pushed Krueger into early retirement. After talking with the wholesaler who sold the goods to Krueger's, Lewis learned of a home improvement company that was growing in North Carolina and expanding into Maryland and Pennsylvania. So they packed up and moved to Philadelphia in 1965 to take an assistant manager job at one of the new stores.

His effort and love for what he did was unmatched. Not only did he strive to just do the job; he always strived to do it better. Over time Lewis continued to move up the ladder and by 1972 was moved to northern Virginia to be assistant store manager and then in 1976 was moved to Richmond to open his own store. They tried to persuade his mother to come, but she wouldn't hear of it. She wished them well and passed away in 1979.

After nine years in Richmond, Sadie was diagnosed with cancer. Lewis took early retirement, cashed in on his stock options which had grown *very* significantly (by then the company had gone nationwide and went from six stores to six hundred stores). Lewis spent a good majority of the next two years either at the medical center by Sadie's side or at the university library down the street—the same library where we met. It was close to the hospital and gave him time to do some volunteer work to take his mind off things. Sadie passed away in 1987.

Even with family still close by (Jacob, 33, was still single and living in Fredericksburg and Danielle, 41, was happily married with a boy, James, and a girl, Rebekah, in high school), Lewis still needed time to take his mind off things and found the library was a great release. But over time, and with Sadie gone, he started missing work. With all that experience and years with warehousing, stock, and inventory an idea came to him one day while re-shelving some library books—an idea for a better system.

With the savings he had left he went into partnership with his accountant son and his computer programming son-in-law and formed Anderson Inventory Systems, a computer software company that built programs for companies to keep track of their stock and sales. With more and more businesses switching over to computer systems and all of his years in the industry he knew exactly what was needed and was able to help other companies catch his vision—and more importantly buy his product.

The company blossomed during the late 80's and early 90's and continued to add client after client. It went from a small family firm of three employees to a legitimate software company staffing over two-hundred before all was said and done. It was a true technology success story. Lewis sold the company in 1994 for an undisclosed amount, was approached by the president of the university to help fund an overhaul of the library with his newfound riches and the rest is history

He received an honorary doctorate in business administration in 1995, continued to volunteer at the library until 1997, and passed away in 1999.

I met Lewis for the first time in 2001 . . . and he changed my life forever.

Read how I first met Lewis in *The Greatest Discovery*.

www.pondpublishing.com

Made in the USA
Middletown, DE
24 August 2019